K.O.'D
IN THE
RIFT

Other books by Victoria Heckman

K.O.'d in Hawai'i Mystery Series:
K.O.'d in Honolulu
K.O.'d in the Volcano

K.O.'d in the Rift

A K.O.'d in Hawai'i Mystery

For Phil —
enjoy your trip to the islands!
Aloha,
Victoria Heckman
7·18·05

Victoria Heckman

PEMBERLEY PRESS

CORONA DEL MAR

PEMBERLEY PRESS
P O Box 1027
Corona del Mar, CA 92625
www.pemberleypress.com
A member of The Authors Studio
www.theauthorsstudio.org

Cover design: Kat & Dog Studios
Cover photo: Gary W. Holmlund
Photo of Victoria Heckman courtesy of:
Blue Moon Photography

Library of Congress Cataloging-in-Publication Data

Heckman, Victoria.
    K.O.'d in the rift / Victoria Heckman.-- 1st North American ed.
        p. cm. -- (A K.O.'d in Hawai'i mystery)
    Summary: "Honolulu Police Officer Katrina Ogden must solve
a murder to prove her boyfriend's innocence, even though she
finds herself opposing him on the issue of Hawaiian
Sovereignty" "[summary]"--Provided by publisher.
    ISBN 0-9702727-7-4 (alk. paper)
    1. Policewomen--Fiction. 2. Police--Hawaii--Honolulu--
Fiction. 3. Honolulu (Hawaii)--Fiction. I. Title: KO'd in the
rift. II. Title.
    PS3608.E296K14 2005
    811'.6--dc22
                                        2005012427

iv

For George Cretton—Rhett
Love, Scarlet

and my sons
Zach and Liam
the lights of my life

Acknowledgements

This is a work of fiction. While the Hawaiian Sovereignty movement is real and part of Hawai'i's history along with the overthrow of the Hawaiian monarchy, to my knowledge there is no Hawaiian Cultural Society or a *Ka Leo O Kanaka* group or movement. All events and characters are fictional and created for the use of the novel.

Mahalo to those without whom I could not have written this: Sgt. Kathleen Osmond, HPD, my partner in crime; Susan Siu, Investigator with the Honolulu Medical Examiner's Office who patiently answered a thousand questions; Pat Ricks of Pemberley Press, Margaret Searles—my lucky charm; George Cretton, whose friendship and kindness stayed with me for over twenty years; and most importantly, my family—without their support and love, nothing would be possible.

Author's Note: The name *Kaneali'ihiwi* roughly translates as *royalty (royal man) of the ridge.*

O ke aloha ke kuleana
o kahi malihini

Love is the host
in strange lands.

CHAPTER ONE

Honolulu police officer Katrina Ogden, "K.O.", sat slumped at her desk, chin in hand, dispiritedly surveying the four foot high stack of paper in the corner.

The Sergeant's Exam study materials.

She had started to study. Several times. It just seemed like something always interrupted her. She did take some of it home to work on late at night after her 3:00 to 11:00 P.M. shift in Evidence. That was the problem—late at night. With the best of intentions, she sat at her dining room table, stiff and uncomfortable, bright light glaring onto the pages. It did no good. She drifted off to sleep and woke hours later with a crick in her neck and no idea of what she'd read.

The exam—designed by a clerk test preparer at the city and county level, not a cop—was nearly impossible to study for. It could encompass anything and everything from union rules to police standards and conduct. It was a "crapshoot," as others gone before had told K.O.

K.O. sighed, rubbed her face and ran her fingers through her short, red hair. This wasn't getting anything done, much less studying for the exam.

She told herself she'd finish checking the forms stacked on her desk against the evidence submitted, then she'd crack the penal code book. Again.

As the head of Evidence on her shift, one of her tasks was to make sure that the evidence logged in, was actually what and where it was said to be. She picked up the log on her way to the Evidence room in the main office.

She unlocked the door and stepped inside the cavernous room. Metal shelves lined the walls up to the ceiling, and more rows divided the room into narrow aisles—a bizarre warehouse of people's lives torn apart by crime.

The room was further divided by types of crime and evidence. Separate sections for weapons, homicide, drugs. Larger pieces of evidence, such as cars, were kept in a different, roomier location.

She passed by a boogie board with a large, jagged semi-circular bite missing. During her first tour of the evidence locker, she'd asked why this obvious, but sinister-looking item was included. It was considered evidence in a Missing Persons case, because a body had never been recovered.

Every time she passed it, she thought, "Duh. He's going to be missing for a long time."

She walked among the shelves, matching tag numbers to items, trying not to absorb the thousands of objects, some bloodied and mangled, others more innocuous looking, that represented unsolved crimes. It saddened her to think that so many cases would never be closed, meaning that all those families touched by them would have no closure. In self-defense she shut them all out, those small voices asking for help, and briskly moved through the shadowy room.

CHAPTER TWO

Seven A.M. found Donna Costello, Chief Death Investigator for the Honolulu Medical Examiner's Office, crawling like a snake down a tunnel barely higher than she was lying down.

Investigator-in-training Ben "Tiny" Sugano scooted parallel several feet away.

Honolulu PD waited outside for the verdict. Two hours earlier, HPD had received a call reporting a body in a cave, discovered by a couple of teenaged boys.

A death investigator was called to the scene of every death, often before the police. The M.E.'s office, in the form of a death investigator, usually determined if detectives should be summoned. HPD on the leeward side had beaten her here since Makaha was nearly an hour's drive west from her office.

By the time Donna and Tiny had arrived, HPD had already sent a reluctant officer in to confirm that there was, in fact, a body. A skeleton to be precise. Upon Donna's and Tiny's arrival, the "body" had escalated to become the victim of a sex crime because the shaken officer thought he had seen remnants of panties and some kind of bludgeon. He had not remained in the cave.

Donna pushed a flashlight ahead of her and scraped forward

using her fingers and toes, feeling her jeans and T-shirt catch unpleasantly on the rough surface.

Donna Costello, a *haole* from the Mainland, had been on the job two years—a long time, particularly for females in the field. A co-worker had committed suicide a few months ago, and even now, Donna pushed the knowledge aside, refusing to deal with it.

At the M.E.'s office, it had been a slow week in terms of bodies. A couple of homeless, a domestic death in Palama, and an infant with congenital birth defects.

Tiny stopped, and his flashlight beam dipped. "I can't go any farther. It's too small. My knees is killin' me."

Sweat poured off him in the confined space. Donna could see it dripping off his nose to form a dark blot on the reddish dirt, even as she felt it run from under her own arms and off her ribs. The air was close and unmoving. The cloying smell of the dirt itself was filled with what she was sure were droppings from various creatures.

She shivered. Give her a dead human body any day over a bunch of rats or bugs. Perhaps that discomfort was what had given way to her eccentric hobby of building "insect death scenes," as she termed them. Some measure of control over creepy crawlies. She took dead insects—the large, Hawaiian flying roaches were particularly good—and formed intricate crime scenes, complete with mini props and police tape.

"Come on, Tiny. Suck it in, brah, you can make it." Donna grunted and shoved herself forward a few inches. "I can see the larger cave. Look." She flashed her light over the walls of a roomy cavern.

"Yeah, yeah, yeah. So you say." Tiny pushed, and with a scraping sound, slithered down a slight slope into the main cave.

Donna followed, her light bouncing off the walls and floor to illuminate what she knew to be a piece of bone. She approached the bundle of dried human bones, desiccated, chipped and cracked. They had been in the cave a long time. With its remnants of ti leaves and other signs, Donna knew the cave was no crime scene, but a sacred, ancient Hawaiian burial site. The "panties" were a ragged pile of tattered kapa cloth, the "bludgeon," a worn-smooth, lava *poi*-pounder. An intimidating potential weapon to be sure, but this one had been used for nothing more sinister than pounding taro root into *poi*—the staple food of the ancient Hawaiian people.

Donna sighed. The cave would remain untouched except for a blessing ceremony, which was performed any time a sacred place was defiled.

The confined space, the draining adrenaline that accompanied each new potential crime scene, and the musty, guano-laden air were getting to her. Donna beckoned to Tiny and they began their painstaking exit from the cave.

Neither of them saw the second body—only days old—that had been forced into a shadow-filled niche.

CHAPTER THREE

The Waikiki Shell bustled with activity as a hundred people set up musical equipment on the stage, stocked food and beer booths, and checked everything from sound to seating. Afternoon sun blazed down on the grassy slope, the ice blue sky devoid of even the wisps of clouds that nearly always capped the emerald Koʻolau mountains.

K.O. sweated in her navy blue, wool-blend uniform, cursing once again the idiocy of wool in Hawaiʻi. She had taken the Special Duty assignment at this Hawaiian Cultural Society fundraising concert to earn some extra bucks. Christmas was only a few months away, and she had a lot of gifts to buy for co-workers and family. Also, she wanted to buy something special for Alani.

Whether he was her "boyfriend" or not, he was certainly important in her life. She smiled as she thought of his large hands, made strong by paddling, his copper skin like silk over work-defined muscles.

Suddenly she was much hotter than she'd been a moment ago.

She strode to a booth, the vendor displaying icy bottles of water.

"Hi, Sam. Can get one water, brah?"

"Sure, K.O." He handed her a bottle. "Nah, nah, nah." He flapped his hands as she tried to hand him two dollars.

"Come on, Sam. You know I can't." K.O. refused freebies, no matter how small. With so many police departments under scrutiny, including her own, she avoided all possibility of complaint in this regard. Probably to an extreme, she decided, looking at Sam's narrowed eyes and downturned mouth.

"K.O., you hurtin' my feelings. We been friends, how long?"

"Yeah, Sam. I know. No make beef, yeah?" Sam continued to stare, arms folded. "And quit da stink eye!"

"You one stubborn *haole*. You know dat?"

"Sure, Sam. I know. You can buy me a beer after work sometime, okay?"

"'Kay, den." Sam smiled, his large, white teeth gleaming. "And, I want interest."

K.O. groaned. "What kine interest?"

"Karaoke!"

"No, way!" K.O. wailed.

"Yeah, way. You might need my help someday. Maybe even today." Sam put his hands in his drooping pockets, assuming an "aw, shucks" posture. "You know, a whole bunch of Hawaiians, all heated up about the Kingdom of Hawai'i, all dis politics stuff. You jus' a little *haole* girl in uniform. One big target, I t'ink, if the *blalas* get all *huhu.*"

"This is a fundraiser for cultural awareness, not a political rally on the merits of Hawaiian Sovereignty. Besides, I'm not such a little *haole* girl, Sam." K.O.'s five-foot-seven frame stood at least two inches taller than the older man's. She smiled. "I get you. Okay, we sing one song. And not 'Summer Nights.' I'm sick of that one. You're going to have to buy me way more than one beer to get me to sing, you know."

"I know." Sam positively smirked, then turned serious. "Fo' reals, K.O. Watch your back tonight. All these guys talking about taking Hawai'i back, ceding from the United States Government.

Sometimes, I don't know. They get so worked up, and you are a *haole.*"

"I know, Sam. Been white all my life. I'm used to it. But tonight's fundraiser is just for the Hawaiian Cultural Society. It'll be fine. HPD is watching the radicals. Chill, Sam."

Sam leaned over the narrow partition and whispered. "I tell you something. Das not all. *Ka Leo O Kanaka* is behind dis fundraiser."

"Are you serious? The 'Voice of the People?' That extreme group that practically wants to go back five hundred years in time?" Sam nodded. "How do you know?"

"I hear t'ings. I hear them say, 'We gonna make a point.' But you didn't hear it from me."

"What kind of 'point?'"

"I don't know. Go now."

Sam suddenly seemed nervous, and his nervousness was catching. K.O. nodded, grabbed her water, and quickly walked away, ostensibly making security checks, but her mind whirled with the implications of this news.

If *Ka Leo O Kanaka* was behind tonight's fundraising concert, that added a whole new and dangerous dimension to a relaxed evening of Hawaiian culture and song.

Nothing had been proved, but this group was said to be responsible for several peaceful demonstrations turning violent, a number of anonymous threats, and random acts of vandalism to city and county property.

Targeting of white-owned businesses, and even Hawaiians who were deemed by the group to be sympathetic to the U.S., was becoming more widespread. A task force had been formed in cooperation with the U.S. military to keep an eye on the group. No charges had been filed, but a list was developing of suspected participants in the extreme faction, many of whom used the legitimate organization of the Hawaiian Cultural Society as a cover. Among the suspects were two of the top officers in the HCS: Kepa

Nahua, the president of the HCS and suspected leader of *Ka Leo*—who, up until now, had seemed reasonable in expressing the concerns of the Hawaiian Cultural Society—and his second in command, Blala Richards. Richards was reputed to be a drafter of the new Hawaiian Constitution on behalf of *Ka Leo O Kanaka* and much more inclined towards action, even violence, as opposed to discussion.

One of the tenets of the new constitution was for all non-Hawaiians to register as aliens. Another urged Hawaiians not to pay taxes to the U.S. government, and still another called for the removal of all U.S. military presence in Hawai'i.

Blala Richards was also one of Hawai'i's most beloved slack-key guitar players. K.O.'s stomach sank as she realized that, of course, he would be here, at a concert fundraiser. *How to completely disregard the obvious,* she thought, disgusted with her omission.

She hadn't heard that the task force would be here. Although her territory in Evidence would not really warrant her being informed specifically, all of HPD was on alert with daily briefings on the radical group's demands and demonstrations. Thinking on it now, she was sure the task force would be present, maybe even undercover. She knew some of the members and began searching in earnest, to tell them what Sam had said.

A breeze off Waikiki Beach penetrated as far as the Shell, and she began to feel cooler. She allowed herself to slow her pace and drained the water bottle. She stopped on the rise facing the stage, and her eyes swept the scene. The large, grassy area where she stood was for picnickers, and soon it would be a sea of reclining bodies and coolers, the happy shouts of children running through the maze mixing with the sweet strains of slack-key guitar and ukulele in the evening air.

At the bottom of the hill were rows of permanent, hard, plastic chairs. K.O. always preferred the grass to the more expensive, closer seats.

The smells of barbeque *kal bi* beef, steamed rice, and stir fry drifted to K.O., making her stomach growl. *Why do I get hungry when I'm nervous?* she wondered idly as she watched some roadies plug in huge amplifiers on either side of the large stage. A few musicians milled about, testing mics and instruments, some tethered by electrical cords, others wandering, twanging and banging discordantly.

K.O. loved these open-air concerts, and although she was nervous now, she was also filled with anticipation. The music of Polynesia always transported her. Listening, she felt both rooted to the land and people, and also freed—flying above the islands, connected by spirit. She shook her head to clear it. She felt a little silly about her esoteric thoughts now, realizing that especially tonight she would have to be vigilant—not let herself go on the wings of song.

A horrible screech of feedback helped focus her. She walked down the slope and behind the large shell-shaped amphitheatre. Another burst of feedback made her scrunch her eyes shut and clap her hands over her ears. She smacked straight into a large, solid body.

She opened her eyes to the massive chest of Blala Richards. His brown eyes stared coldly at her and his large hands grasped her by the shoulders, thrusting her away. Her bones ached under his grip.

"Watch yourself," he said, still imprisoning her. Wavy, dark hair flowed nearly to his waist, and his wild facial tattoos served their purpose—a flash of fear shuddered through her, leaving a metallic taste in her mouth.

The ancient Hawaiians revered size. The larger the person, the more powerful, the more mana.

Richards's mana was as tangible as a suit of armor.

Any authority she might have had was lost, as she stood so near him, she could feel the heat of his body and his barely contained wildness. Even as defensive moves raced through her brain, she knew, with his intimidating size and weight, he could snap her neck and she wouldn't be able to stop him.

He released her abruptly. She stumbled—free of whatever spell had held her. "It's a dangerous place, backstage." He moved away, graceful and soundless—a tiger in his jungle element—at home and extremely dangerous.

K.O. staggered to a folding chair and collapsed, trying to get air into her tortured lungs. She had been holding her breath. She had never experienced his kind of power before. In her job, she had felt fear, but Richards's feralness—so disdainful of her, so unpredictable—frightened her. She had the feeling he could kill her with no more remorse or consideration than she would have for a roach. It reminded her of people on PCP—immense strength derived from the drug, without values or regard for human life. Blala Richards, however, was clearly not high, but driven by two thousand years of warrior ancestors.

For the first time since K.O. had heard about the newest wave in the Hawaiian Sovereignty movement, she felt she understood what she—they—the "Establishment"—the U.S. Government—was up against. It felt like war. And she was pretty sure this would be a bloody one—one that nobody would win.

CHAPTER FOUR

For the second time in as many days, Donna Costello and Tiny Sugano from the M.E.'s office crawled down the tight tunnel to the sacred burial cave.

They had received a report of a body in the cave. Again. Although Donna had logged and explained the previous circumstances, procedure dictated that she must return and re-investigate. This time, the callers had been professors from the University of Hawai'i at Manoa, and she was forced to leave her other cases.

"At least we know what the cave is like," she grumbled to Tiny as she reached the main cave and creaked upright.

"Yeah. Goody." Tiny beamed his light around and slapped the fine dust from his pants, creating a "Pig Pen" cloud.

Donna coughed. "Thanks, eh, brah?"

"Gee, looks da same to me. What chu t'ink?" Tiny said sarcastically.

"I don't want to come back a third time. Look around good. What they said about a second cave?"

"Somet'ing like dat. Cheez." Tiny stomped around the periphery, his light bouncing wildly.

Donna stood still, watching Tiny with an amused smile. Then, "Stop!" she shouted, startling Tiny into halting.

"What? Like give me one heart attack?" Sweat trickled down his cheek, making a thin, clean track.

Donna walked to where Tiny waited. "Look, but don't move."

"If it's some kinda bug for your collection, man, you on your own . . . " Tiny began.

Donna pointed her flashlight into a small cave several feet away, the entrance previously hidden by shadow. Her light illuminated a shoe. Not an ancient article of footwear, but a modern, blue and white athletic shoe, with a foot in it.

"Crime scene," Donna whispered.

"I know. Oh, man."

"Go get the stuff. Call homicide and S.I.S."

"Yeah, yeah, yeah." Tiny carefully exited the cave and soon returned with the investigative kits.

For the next hour Donna and Tiny photographed, documented, drew, and collected samples. When Detective Rolipsky, a small *haole* investigator from homicide, and Kimo, the ID tech from the Scientific Investigation Section, arrived, Tiny scooted out, and they slithered in to collect their own set of photos and samples.

Detective Rolipsky sat back on his heels. "Now what?"

Donna wiped her filthy face with her equally filthy T-shirt. "Gotta get him out."

"I was afraid you were gonna say that."

They had already not only examined the male victim in his niche, but also extracted his body and done a preliminary exam on the cave floor. He had been shot—dead several days, and rigor come and gone. No wallet or ID, but he looked familiar to Donna. More photos and documentation followed, but additional detail would have to wait until the full autopsy at the office. Donna had mentally kicked herself for missing the victim on the previous visit and wondered what shit would roll downhill on her from her boss.

In the end, they ran a collapsible stretcher under the corpse and pulled it with straps from its resting place into the bright Hawaiian sun.

Light glinted off the cobalt sea fronting Makaha beach; the cleansing breeze brought her the distant shouts and laughs of surfers below. Donna stretched on the trail outside the cliff cave entrance and allowed herself a moment of mourning for the victim.

He had not been killed in the cave, but had been brought here, at great risk and considerable difficulty. He was *haole*. This was a place sacred to Hawaiian people and had, therefore, been defiled by his body.

Had that been intentional? She shook her head. It wasn't her problem to solve homicides. But something about this one bothered her. Certain things just didn't add up.

Roly and Tiny loaded the body into the M.E.'s van. With a last glance at the horizon, Donna got into the driver's seat while Tiny rode shotgun. They drove east in unaccustomed silence. Donna wondered what she was missing about the crime scene while Tiny picked at a hole in his pants, eyes on the ocean.

CHAPTER FIVE

K.O. saw other Special Duty officers as she wandered through the Waikiki Shell grounds, looking for any task force members. Although she mentioned *Ka Leo* to them, none of them seemed concerned or had heard anything suspicious.

The Shell began to fill with excited fans. Families spread blankets and pre-show music blared over the PA. Everything seemed normal, and K.O. tried to relax. The afternoon was perfect. Clear sky, waving palms, tropical breeze. Why was she so nervous?

She had left the backstage area immediately after running into Blala. Her throat went dry again just thinking about the encounter. What had happened?

Nothing, she told herself. *I'm just paranoid.*

The music cut out and a roar went up from the audience. On stage was a popular DJ from KCCN, the Hawaiian radio station. K.O. couldn't hear him clearly, but the audience laughed and clapped. She moved closer and heard him welcoming the crowd and announcing the first act. She moved through the booths, which now did brisk business.

The first band took up positions on stage and launched into a fast song accompanied by much howling and clapping from the audience. K.O. saw a group of shirtless young men standing near the stage. They seemed rowdier than the surrounding families. She also noticed that the American flag was absent from the stage. Only the Hawaiian flag flew.

As she worked her way towards the *malo*-clad men, she saw that many people in the crowd carried or wore Hawaiian flags. Her twinge of unease went up a notch. The second number was in progress, and a lovely young woman joined the band on stage. Her long *holoku* clung to her slim frame as she swayed in a traditional hula.

"Scuse me, brah," K.O. said to the nearest young man.

Hawaiian tattoos banded his chiseled body. Along his breast bone, like a black necklace, was inked the legend "Hawaiian Pride—Hawaiian Strength," above a warrior image that bounced and twitched as his chest muscles contracted.

"What?" he said belligerently seeing K.O.'s uniform.

At least, K.O. hoped it was the uniform. *It's a sad day when both my job and my skin color are wrong,* she thought.

Living in Hawai'i for almost twenty years had taught her a lot about racial tolerance, among other things. The last few years, however, she had seen an escalation in the Hawaiian Sovereignty issue. Previously a non-issue, as some would term it, the unrest in the native Hawaiian population regarding the 1896 overthrow of the Hawaiian Monarchy was rapidly turning into a civil war.

K.O. had tried to follow the arguments, see both sides. She still didn't understand it. She had read the letters, articles, the documentation. She had been on duty during some of the speeches and rallies. The anger over the usurping of Hawaiian lands, off-set by public pacification in the form of more speeches and apologies by both churches and some U.S. Government heads, only seemed to make things worse.

The whole thing made her nervous because she couldn't see a solution. Certain groups and individuals, like the radical *Ka Leo,* for one, didn't seem to want a peaceful resolution. Reverting to a monarchy for Hawai'i, seceding from the U.S., sounded like what the group was after. Was that the right thing for the Hawaiian people? Was that even possible?

K.O. didn't know. She lived here. She loved it here. She was sworn to uphold the law—but laws could change. She was *haole.* White.

Back to her skin color versus her job.

"Hey, brah," she told the man. "You folks can sit down, please? You blocking da view fo' da little kids."

The young man puffed up a little. He mad-dogged her—waged a staring match—for a few seconds, then glanced at the families seated behind his group. He slapped his nearest friend. "Alika, brah. Let's sit. Tired of standing, yeah?"

His friend turned and also eyed K.O. Then he slapped another buddy, until they were all staring at her.

She stood straight and authoritative, but her heart hammered. She did not want to be the start of a riot. K.O. chose to interpret their attention as agreement. "Thanks, eh, brah. I'm sure they appreciate it."

She nodded, the short, upward bob of the head that can mean anything from "yes" to "hello." In this case, she meant, "thanks."

The first young man bobbed back. "You're welcome." He slowly sat, and the rest of the men did, too.

K.O. stepped to the side, and continued down the slope to *"da luas,"* the port-a-potties. Her adrenaline was pumping, and she felt as if she might be sick. Entering a *lua* might help that right along, she thought, but she didn't want to throw up in front of an audience.

She slammed open a door and entered, locking it quickly, breathing rapidly. The chemical smell wasn't too bad, and the breeze through the upper screens cooled the interior.

She didn't throw up, but she wondered what the hell was happening here. Happening to her?

"Get your shit together, girl. You gonna be *haole* your whole

CHAPTER SEVEN

A gang-related shooting in Kalihi had pushed back Donna Costello's schedule. She had worked late to finish examining those bodies as well as the man from the cave. She washed her hands and trudged upstairs to her office to complete the paperwork. The phone rang.

"Costello."

"Good news and bad news. Whaddya want first?" asked Tiny Sugano, her assistant.

"Not in the mood, Tiny. Just tell me. I'm wiped." Donna eased off her shoes and slid her feet onto the desk, stretching her toes.

"I might have an ID on that John Doe from da cave."

"Yeah? Who?"

"Missing person. Reported three days ago, missing for four."

The time frame sounded right to Donna. "Anyone come forward to make a positive ID? Who is it, anyway?"

"You can look at last week's paper, fo' dat."

"What do you mean?" Donna pulled her feet down and held her head.

"Larry Ellis."

"Shit. No." High profile. The spokesman for the Lt. Governor's office and the primary liaison for the State of Hawai'i vs. Hawaiian Sovereignty issue. Supposedly, what Ellis said in any meeting or negotiation meant it came from the state government, in the form of the Lt. Governor's office, which in turn was influenced by the Federal government. *Shit.*

"That's just great. I take it, that's the bad news?"

"So far." Tiny sounded almost cheerful.

"What? What else you got. Don't hold out on me, man. I'm so tired, I'm seeing double."

"'Kay, den. Know who reported him missing?"

"Tiny . . . ." Her voice dropped threateningly.

"All right, already. Cheez, lighten up! Not da wife. Not da Lt. Gov's office. You like guess?"

"Tiny!"

"Kepa Nahua, da president of da Hawaiian Cultural Society!"

"Why would he do that?"

"He piss off. Ellis missed like two meetings in a row. I guess, some kine negotiations or somethin' li' dat. Anyway, Kepa called to complain to the Lt. Governor's office. Said it was gon' look bad that da State denying da people, blah, blah. So, some temporary sackatary don' know what da hell's goin' on, gets all da kine and tells him, wait—I wrote 'em down."

Donna sighed during the paper shuffling.

"Try wait, you gon' like dis." Tiny's voice went up an octave, and he assumed a *haole* accent. "'This is the Lt. Governor's Office, not the Missing Persons Bureau. I suggest you call the police and make a Missing Persons report. Good day.' Good day! I love dat. So, Kepa did. And boy, he all samurai about it, too. He didn't jus' call in. He went down there. Choice, yeah?"

"Yeah. Choice." Donna's head swirled with the implications of this news. The political climate was dicey enough without this. Wasn't a sovereignty rally scheduled tomorrow at Fort Street Mall downtown?

The news would get out. It always did. A man murdered—

and not just any man. The white man negotiating with the Hawaiian Cultural Society for Hawaiian Homelands on behalf of the State of Hawai'i, and who knew else? Maybe even for the U.S. Government.

Jeez, the Office of Hawaiian Affairs, OHA, was probably in there, too, she realized. She wished she'd paid more attention to the news.

The victim found in a sacred Hawaiian burial cave. Reported missing by the head of the HCS, which everyone knew was really *Ka Leo o Kanaka.* Practically the Hawaiian mob.

"Oh, God. I knew I should have taken my vacation this month." Donna folded her arms on her desk and rested her head on them, eyes closed. Without looking, she groped for the phone, hearing her coffee mug slither off the desk and shatter, spilling the tepid brew.

Still with her head on the desk, she punched in a well-known number. After three rings, Homicide detective Rolipsky answered.

"Costello, here. M.E.'s office. I got good news and bad news. Whaddya want first?"

CHAPTER EIGHT

K.O. drove home after her Special Duty assignment at the Shell, thankful that nothing else dire had happened after the amplifier incident. A bunch of people had gotten drunk as usual, but at least they were happy drunks, she thought. No fist fights. Even that group of young punks had not caused any problems.

She peeled off her uniform, stiff with sweat, and headed for the shower. Teresa, her rescued tabby cat, followed her into the bathroom, conversing loudly. To K.O. the noise was music, but she was sure Teresa was complaining about the room service.

"I promise, after my shower, crunchies for days." K.O. scratched Teresa behind the ears and heard purring even over the running water.

A hot shower, and a bourbon and Diet Pepsi later, K.O. felt revived. She sat in her living room with the blinds open. Her second floor unit on the windward side of the island faced the beautiful Ko'olau mountains. The moon was high, and she saw the cardboard cutout shape of the ridge line, sharp and distinct. During the day, the lush greens blended with the clouds and looked like a fairy castle should sit up there.

Through her open lanai door, the wet, tropical smell of rotting foliage wafted in, and she inhaled deeply, finding the odor soothing.

A muted rush reached her ears. One of her favorite sounds—rain. Soft at first, it soon became a pounding roar that sent drops splashing sideways into her house. The fresh, clean smell and encompassing sound worked their magic, washing away the remnants of her difficult evening.

At last she felt she could sleep. She locked her lanai, picked up Teresa and settled into bed. Teresa took her usual spot on the empty pillow next to K.O.'s.

Briefly, before she drifted off, K.O. wondered if Alani would ever use that pillow.

* * *

Early morning sun streamed through K.O.'s open blinds. Hot and yellow, the streaks fell like ribbons, turning her bedroom the color of an Easter egg.

She stretched luxuriously. Despite her late night and stressful duty, she felt rested and ready to get up.

She wandered to the kitchen and started the coffee maker. Teresa's bowl was empty. "Where're you putting it all, girl?"

Teresa sat mute and demure at K.O.'s feet; the picture of feline innocence and propriety. K.O. poured more kibble, then went into the bathroom. The coffee was done, and she poured a cup, inhaling the Kona Mac Nut aroma. She sat in her favorite recliner, watching the mountains once again.

Into the peace, the phone intruded. K.O. debated answering, but in the end, picked up.

"Katrina, darling!" Hardly anyone called her Katrina—just family, and—oh, no. *Abby.* Her mother's ancient bridge-playing friend from Seattle.

"Katrina, you darling girl! How the heck are you?"

Oh, good. And her equally ancient husband, Richard-the-letch on the extension. This could not be good.

"Hi, Abby; Richard. How are you?"

"Oh, fine, dear! We have a surprise for you!" Abby said.

Oh, no. "Oh, great. What?" Abby's and Richard's last surprise was to show up unannounced on their vacation to Hawai'i and drag K.O. to a commercial luau.

"We're back!" said Richard.

"Back where?" K.O. asked cautiously.

"Here, silly! In the 'Land of Aloha!'"

Oh, God. Now what? Another luau was probably too much to hope for. "Uh, why? I mean, you folks were just here. Weren't you?"

"That was ages ago!" It seemed like just yesterday to K.O. "We loved it so much we decided to buy!" *Abby.*

"Buy what?"

"A condo." *Richard.* "And the best part is, we'll be here lots, so we can visit!"

I should just slit my wrists right now. "Wow. That is news. Where is your condo?" *Please, please, please, not the windward side.*

"Where is it again, Richard?"

"Just a minute, honey bunch, I have the brochure right here. Starts with a W."

Please, please, please.

"Here we are. Waikiki Tradewinds."

Thank you, thank you. Waikiki was just about as far from K.O.'s place as was possible. "Great! That's really great!"

"I knew you'd be thrilled! Doesn't she sound thrilled, Richard?"

"Yessiree, Bob. And to celebrate, we're taking you out to lunch, and we won't take no for an answer."

"I have to work today."

"Yes, but you have to eat!" Abby said.

"And if you don't come to us, we'll come to you," added Richard.

K.O. knew this was no empty threat. Abby and Richard at the police station. *Fantastic.* "Oh, no. I'll come to you. Where would you like to meet? Your new place?"

"That sounds Jim Dandy, honey. We don't really know many

places around here, but we will! You betcha," said Richard.

That sounded like a threat if K.O. ever heard one. "Great. I'll meet you in front of the Waikiki Tradewinds at noon. I can see your condo, and then we can eat. Does that sound all right?"

"Oh, I'm so excited," Abby said. "Katrina, we've never seen your place! I know we haven't spent much time in the islands before, but now that's going to change. When are we going to see your beautiful little townhouse?"

When my dead and decaying body is scraped out of here with a spatula. "Oh, soon. I'll have to have you folks over real soon. Gotta go. See you at noon."

K.O. hung up, exhausted once again. It was 7:52 A.M. She still had a ton of things to do. Now, with even less time to do them before her afternoon shift began.

She carefully rearranged Teresa in the recliner and rose.

She was pulling on her jeans when the phone rang again.

No, not them again. It's not fair.

"Hello?"

"K.O., it's Sue Akua. We're having a special meeting before shift today. Come at two for an extra briefing on the Sovereignty Task Force developments. The shit's hitting the fan and everyone's being updated. We're gonna be pulling overtime and Special Duty for days."

"What shit, what fan?" K.O. struggled to hear as she pulled a T-shirt over her head.

"For one, a homicide that's probably going to knock this whole sovereignty negotiation on its ear. The Lt. Governor's liaison to the Hawaiian Cultural Society turned up dead yesterday. Homicide thinks *Ka Leo* had something to do with it, but a whole lot of stuff about it doesn't make sense."

"What stuff?"

"He was found in a burial cave, for one."

"Wow!" K.O. tied her tennis shoes. "Wait. You're right. That doesn't make sense. Would *Ka Leo* do that to their own site?"

"Yeah, I know. It's anybody's guess right now. Nobody's talking. More at the briefing. You working the Fort Street Mall demonstration?"

"I didn't sign up for Special Duty. Do they need more officers?"

"Dunno, but they're pulling all kinds of folks from all shifts and departments for it."

"Sounds like somebody's getting nervous." K.O. grabbed her purse and jacket, grateful again for a cordless phone.

"Uncle Sam, for one. I overheard a conversation and a whole lot of somebodies are nervous."

"I just had an interesting experience at the Shell last night that tells me this thing is way bigger than they're telling us."

"I'm getting that idea, too. Gotta go, K.O. They're paging me."

"Thanks, Sue. See you later."

K.O. hung up and picked up Teresa one last time. "You hold down the fort here, okay?" Teresa's unblinking gaze met hers and she leaned forward until her nose touched K.O.'s. Then she chirrupped. Both the sound and gesture were what she used to do to her young kittens, before they were adopted.

K.O. laughed. "I'll be fine. Just in case, I'll get you more crunchies, okay?" She put a second bowl next to the first. "You look positively smug."

Teresa didn't comment as K.O. went out the door.

CHAPTER NINE

K.O. rushed through her errands—picking up her dry-cleaned uniforms, returning library books, shopping—and then pulled into the yellow zone in front of the Waikiki Tradewinds at three minutes to noon. Richard and Abby were just tottering out of the lobby. They looked even more frail than when she'd last seen them.

She felt a twinge of guilt at her attitude towards them. After all, they were her mother's closest friends in Seattle. K.O. rolled down the passenger window and shut off the engine. "Should I park and see your place, or do you want to eat first?"

Richard leaned in. "Let's drive to the Sizzler. Abby loves their cheese toast. I could use a juicy steak myself." Richard smacked his lips and a drop of saliva spattered onto K.O.'s upholstery.

K.O. wiped it off with a tissue. *Yuck.* "Okay by me. Let me help you." She hurried around the car to assist Abby into the back seat. She was dismayed to see Richard slam the back door and open the front passenger door. K.O. sighed and began moving her files, her books, her king-size Mag-lite flashlight, and a collection of AD/DC and Judas Priest cassette tapes. Her trunk was already full of non-perishable groceries and kitty litter, along with her blue roof bubble.

K.O.'s silver-grey Crown Victoria was also her police vehicle, subsidized by the department. It was equipped with radio, siren, and the removable roof rack with the blue police bubble.

Richard collapsed heavily into the seat, and she heard a crunch as her one and only Scorpions tape case splintered under his behind. Fortunately, the tape itself was in the car's player, and she took petty satisfaction in knowing the hard rock music would blast as soon as she turned on the ignition.

She had to drive a considerable distance around several blocks to get to the Sizzler's parking lot on the odd-shaped corner of Kalakaua and Ala Moana streets. Although it was only a few minutes' walk from the condo, she doubted Abby could have made it.

After Richard had ordered half the meat on the menu and they settled at a table, K.O. turned the discussion to their purchase. "How did you find your condo?"

"It was the strangest thing," Abby began. "Remember when we visited here last and we had that lovely time at the luau?"

Vividly. Painfully. "Yes, of course." K.O. sipped her water and held her tongue.

"Well, one day when we went for a walk, the nicest young man asked us if we wanted a free case of macadamia nuts! Isn't that the strangest thing you ever heard?"

Not really, but K.O. suddenly had a bad feeling about the direction the conversation was taking. "What happened next?"

"I asked what the catch was, because I know nothing's free in this world," Richard said.

"So what was the catch?" K.O. asked, but she already knew.

"We just had to listen to an hour's presentation on buying a condo here in Hawai'i!" Abby said.

"It was such a good deal, we couldn't pass it up," Richard added.

"So you bought one?" K.O. asked weakly.

"We sure did, honey. Best deal I ever made. For just a few

thousand down and some maintenance fees, we got ourselves a little piece of paradise. So we can visit you any time we like! Ahhh . . . here we go," Richard said as several plates were placed before him.

K.O. had ordered the salad bar, but had waited until Abby's and Richard's food arrived to fill her plate. Now her appetite was gone.

"Richard. Abby. You do realize you bought a timeshare condo, don't you?"

"Course we do! That's what's so great. We don't have to do a thing." Richard sawed into his steak.

"Richard, a timeshare means you only get it at your time of the year, unless you buy or negotiate additional weeks. You don't get it 'any time you want.'"

"Course we do. The man said. It's in the papers we signed."

"Do you happen to have those papers with you?" K.O. asked, feeling worse by the minute. It was one thing that Richard and Abby got on her nerves, but another for someone to take advantage of them. She knew how poorly Richard could see. He was nearly as bad as her mother, who was legally blind. Abby's vision was better, but K.O. doubted if Abby could understand the legalese of these timeshare operators' contracts. K.O. was sure that Abby had not read the whole thing aloud to Richard.

"I have everything back at the room."

"Richard, I don't want to make you folks nervous, but I have a feeling you may not have purchased what you thought you did." K.O. continued explaining how timeshares worked. Granted, some of them were legitimate, but many of the companies had been brought up on charges of fraud, among other things, and the losers were always the clients who purchased the equivalent of the Brooklyn Bridge.

K.O.'s heart sank as she saw their happy faces turn more glum with each of her sentences. Abby's lips trembled, and Richard pushed his half-eaten lunch away.

Anger burned inside K.O. She wanted to run out of the restaurant and find the bastard who'd sold them this whole farce.

"I may be wrong, but let's get those papers and see what it is you agreed to, okay?"

"There he is!" Abby said, pointing across the dining room.

"There who is?" K.O. was confused by the rapid change of topic.

"The man who explained it all to us. Isn't that right, darling? Richard, look."

"I'm not sure," Richard hesitated. K.O. knew he was self-conscious about his diminishing vision and independence. Much of his bluster came from hiding his self-perceived weakness.

She softened suddenly, feeling a swell of tenderness for this fiercely loving and independent, but obviously fragile couple. She turned to see a local-looking man in his thirties, eating alone. "Abby, are your sure? What's his name?"

"Kepa. Right, Richard?"

"Yes. Kepa. The young man on the street gave us directions to the briefing and said we'd get our macadamia nuts just for listening. This Kepa was the one presenting the units for sale. He's the one who told us everything and gave us the contract." Richard's blue eyes grew watery, and he blew his nose loudly. K.O. looked away. "I'm such a fool."

Abby laid a wrinkled, bird-like hand on his arm. "Richard. Don't. Even if what Katrina said is true. It's all right. Really."

She patted his hand lovingly, and K.O. envied them for a moment. What they had. What they shared. It gave her resolve impetus, and she was halfway across the dining room before she realized it.

She stood over the man's table. "Are you Kepa from the Waikiki Tradewinds timeshares?"

"Yes, I am. Are you interested?"

K.O. sat opposite him in the booth. "I definitely am interested. You sold my friends a condo. The elderly couple over there. And from what they've told me, they have no idea what they've signed or agreed to. They think they've bought a whole condo, not one lousy week a year for how many years? Look at them! They're old and frail. They'll be lucky to make it back next year!" K.O. was so angry her hands shook and she put them in her lap. To keep from shouting, she kept lowering her voice until it was a hiss.

Kepa looked alarmed.

"Elder fraud is a serious crime, and we don't take it lightly here."

"Now wait a minute." Kepa held up a hand. "I explained every detail to them, as I do to all my clients. Everything's in writing. It's a contract. They could read every word before they signed."

"Did you know Richard can barely read a stop sign, his eyesight is so bad? That maybe Abby can read, but she would have no idea what she's reading? Unless you 'explained' it to her."

"That's not my problem. I didn't force them to sign. They wanted to! Besides, they could have brought the contract to a lawyer if they'd wanted.

""Oh, really? I just bet. And you didn't tell them that this offer was for today only, while they were there in the briefing, because—gee! So many folks wanted to buy, you just couldn't hold it for them? That they'd be taking a chance if they left and came back? You couldn't promise a thing—these units just sell themselves?" K.O. saw she was right when Kepa seemed to deflate, then rally.

"They still signed, and you'll have to prove they didn't know what they were signing."

"Oh, I don't think that will be too hard. I have friends in Vice, White Collar Crime, Major Crimes & Lock up, CID, Homicide, and just about everywhere. My card." She stood and flipped her HPD business card on the table. "Call me sometime. Or I'll be calling you." She strode back to Abby and Richard.

"Let's go. We need to get out of here. I have to get to work." K.O.'s hands still shook as she assisted Abby out of the booth.

As they made their way slowly to the parking lot, Richard

pulled a business card from his wallet. "I don't have the papers on me, but I do still have that man's business card, if that will help."

K.O. took the card and her stomach flip-flopped as she read. "Kepa Nahua-Sales Associate, Waikiki Tradewinds, Inc."

CHAPTER TEN

K.O. briefly toured Richard's and Abby's unremarkable unit in the Tradewinds timeshares. She took the papers Richard had given her, agreeing to check them.

She changed into her fresh uniform in the women's locker room at the station, then hustled into the briefing room. Nodding to fellow officers, she grabbed a spot at one of the back tables. She set her notepad out and anxiously twiddled her pen, waiting for the meeting to begin.

The memory of running into Blala Richards at the Shell fundraising concert flowed sharply through her, like an alcohol buzz on an empty stomach.

A handsome, heavyset Hawaiian man in uniform, stood at the podium and held up one hand. The conversation ceased.

"I'm Lieutenant Kiaha, currently assigned to the task force dealing with the *Ka Leo*/Hawaiian Cultural Society political issue. I'm here to brief you on the situation, and for some of you, to change your duty, at least temporarily. We're short on security for upcoming events. Now that it appears the conflict between the U.S. Government and the Hawaiian Sovereignty movement is taking a more violent turn, we feel prevention should be the focus."

K.O. glanced around the room. It appeared this was not news to many officers. Although Oʻahu was a small island, the all-consuming job in any particular department of HPD did tend to isolate personnel as to the bigger picture. With the almost daily protests, rallies, speeches and just plain stunts in the name of publicity, however, K.O. wondered how anyone could remain uninformed. She tuned in just as the lieutenant brought up the murder.

"The word is already out. We knew it couldn't stay under wraps, but we'd hoped to keep it quiet at least until after today's rally at Fort Street Mall."

An older officer raised his hand. "I nevah hear about dis murder, so how da word get out?" Other officers nodded in agreement.

"We're not sure. Could have been from the M.E.'s office, but we doubt it. They're tight up there. Next is Homicide, but again, we doubt it. So, probably the person or persons responsible for the homicide is the best guess. We suspect a radical member of *Ka Leo,* but again, we're not sure. Too many things don't make sense, and we don't have enough information."

The lieutenant paused and studied the room, seeming to take in each and every officer. K.O. felt distinctly uncomfortable as his gaze rested on her face, and she knew he was memorizing hers as well as everyone else's. Not a good feeling to be scrutinized this way. K.O. doodled on her pad and averted her eyes until he finished his sweep. *Chicken skin.* She rubbed at the goose bumps on her pale arms until they receded.

The lieutenant continued. "I have a list of officers I've added to the duty roster for the sovereignty demonstration today. Until further notice, you will report to me, as task force security. When not specifically assigned to task force projects, you will be at the station during your regular shift. Those who normally patrol, will be assigned to the station. You are to be available at a moment's notice, at all times, during your shift. This whole thing could blow up in our faces at any moment, and we will be ready. Understood?"

A mumble of assent.

"The following officers are assigned to me until further notice. And please stay here. If I don't read your name, you are dismissed to your regular duty."

Kiaha read a dozen names, but K.O. only heard her own. The majority of the officers, both uniformed and plainclothes, left the room and K.O. glanced around at the others who remained.

Kiaha sat on the edge of the front table. "Everybody move up."

K.O. shuffled up to the front with the rest.

"We got more than you guys, so no worries, but you da new troops, so you get the background. The others been working dis for a coupla weeks, so they veterans by now."

A few grim smiles. K.O. wished desperately for a Diet Pepsi. Stress made her sleepy and she wanted a caffeine boost. No luck.

Kiaha explained the background of the task force and the role K.O. and the others would play. Like Special Duty, they would be extra security for the rallies and demonstrations. What K.O. hadn't known, was the level of security required, and the threats and problems gone before.

A car bomb parked in front of the judicial building on King Street. Unexploded due to faulty engineering—but Kiaha said they couldn't count on that again. Feds everywhere since several threats against the government had come by mail. The military crawling all over because of the sovereignty debate—overt gestures of apology by the government, while every agency K.O. could think of from FBI to ATF had "people" lurking in every corner.

It's a wonder we're not all bumping into each other as we skulk down some street or another. K.O. conjured up old spy movie footage in her head, but quickly focused again as Kiaha detailed the task force's interaction with the many other agencies involved.

Jeez, you can't tell the players without a program, K.O. thought. If it weren't so horrible, it'd be a comedy.

A uniform brought in a duffel bag and slapped it on the table.

"What you requested, sir."

"Thanks." Kiaha unzipped the duffel and brought out riot gear. "From now on, you go nowhere without this. I know you all wear your vests at all times." Here, he glanced around and several people squirmed.

On a few, K.O. could see the lack of the tell-tale broadening and flattening due to a bulletproof vest.

"But you *will* wear them, and you *will* have this equipment. Check yours out immediately after this briefing. Questions?"

K.O.'s brain reeled with new information, half a dozen questions, and the overwhelming feeling that her corner of paradise was about to explode—might never be the same—and there was not one damn thing she could do about it.

CHAPTER ELEVEN

Unmarked vans dropped numerous personnel on the edges of downtown and in the Fort Street Mall. K.O. was assigned to the north end of the Mall, near Beretania Street. The stage for the rally was set up near the King Street end. K.O. hoped it wouldn't all go to shit.

It became a game for her to observe and see if she could figure out which folks were supporters, and which were some form of undercover agent. Many, like her, were in HPD or HFD uniform and, therefore, easy to spot. A few suits had ear pieces. One homeless man she knew was Vice, but she didn't approach him to find out if he was here acting as Vice or task force. She also included a sweep of "who looks like trouble." A few potentials, but no one obvious. Finally, she gave up as the sun dropped and boredom became the immediate adversary.

The Mall filled until she felt suffocated. She'd had no concept of the degree of interest the sovereignty idea generated.

Distantly, she heard the public address system test and begin to announce the evening's activities. Her stomach dropped as the murder was announced, and a heartfelt speech began about how *Ka Leo* would be framed for the murder of Larry Ellis. She was glad she'd brought her heavy jacket, although carrying it earlier had been a pain.

The wind picked up and whipped down the alley created by the shops and businesses in the open air mall. The crowd pressed closer, and she pressed with them, her eyes not on the stage, but sweeping the crowd.

As the Hawaiian sky darkened and the chill deepened, she felt a sense of aloneness when she could not identify any police officers near her. She was the only *haole* in sight. A nagging thought popped up. What if this whole crowd just turned on her? Or on any fair-skinned person they found? In their enthusiasm, their hatred, their perception of wrong, they just turned on her?

What would she do?

Be torn to ribbons, she thought. The idea also angered her, because she had always supported the Hawaiian people, except the lawbreakers. *I'll go down fighting,* she thought.

"Hey." A soft voice interrupted her internal battle, and she turned, ready to mace, fight, run, whatever.

"Alani!" She wanted to hug him, but her professional restraints interposed. He looked wonderful, tall and bronze in the portable lights of the rally. "What are you doing here?"

"I told the Cultural Society I would be here to show my support."

"Support of what?"

He just looked at her.

"Oh, yeah." He was nearly full-blooded Hawaiian and dedicated to the plight and future of his people. Somehow, when K.O. was with him, he was just Alani, and they were just . . . connected.

"K.O., what's going on?"

"Nothing, yet. I'm here as security. Violence has escalated, and every agency has a finger in the pie." For the first time, it occurred to K.O. that they might not be on the same side after all. At least, not officially.

It saddened her. "I guess . . . I mean . . . ." She looked at him, his features unclear in light and shadow, and resisted an urge to touch his face.

"K.O., I have to do what I believe. The voice of the people will be heard. Remember that." He did more than touch her face. He leaned in for the gentlest of kisses and was gone.

The electrifying touch of his lips seared through her.

Then the impact of his words hit. "The voice"—did he mean *Ka Leo?* Or was he just using a popular phrase? *Oh, God.* She could lose him over this. She hadn't even been sure she'd really wanted him until now. So far, it had been fantasy-dating—no real world intervention. Both on their best behavior; seeing each other only when convenient.

A complete fantasy, she scolded herself in disgust. So what? It wasn't real, and never had been. She turned her attention to the speaker on stage, and turned her sadness into anger, adding it to her earlier emotion—fierce and burning. She wanted a fight.

And she got one—less than an hour later.

Kepa Nahua, flanked by Blala Richards, had the microphone. K.O. pushed her way closer to the stage. The density of the crowd made it difficult to maneuver. Her uniform and her skin color made it even more difficult, but now she didn't care.

"Why would the U.S. Congress apologize to the Hawaiian people if it felt that it had done nothing wrong?"

As Kepa made this statement, she paused. A roar went up, and she realized this was the tail end of a longer speech. The inflamed crowd began a rhythmic chanting and rocking. She tried to move off to the side but was trapped by heaving bodies.

"I quote Queen Liliuokalani herself! 'Oh, honest Americans, as Christians, hear me for my downtrodden people! Their form of government is as dear to them as yours is precious to you. Quite as warmly as you love your country, so they love theirs.' What does that mean to you, my friends? Are we not of one *ohana?* One family against our oppressors?"

K.O. forced herself to remain calm and took out her baton, using it to prod more reluctant fans out of the way. She had just reached the edge of the crowd and was mashed against a glass store front when Kepa made his closing remarks.

"Again, I quote our sovereign, Queen Liliuokalani, 'The cause of Hawai'i and independence is larger and clearer than the life of any man connected with it. Love of country is deep-seated in the breast of every Hawaiian, whatever his station.' Keep these words in your heart and go forth against all who oppose our right to sovereignty!"

The crowd—passionate to begin with—roared its approval. K.O. sensed the moment the tide turned. As soon as Kepa was whisked offstage, enthusiastic supporters screaming his words searched out targets they deemed part of the "oppressors" regime.

That included all personnel in uniform, both HPD and HFD. As K.O. was swept into the melee, she had the brief but ironic thought that many of the "oppressors" in uniform were Hawaiian themselves. Then she just fought to survive.

CHAPTER TWELVE

The next day's edition of the *Honolulu Advertiser* termed it a riot.

K.O. called it hell.

Grimly she recalled the riot gear they had all left in the vans. Whose stupid idea had that been? Once the crowd had gone ballistic, there had been no way to get the protective gear to the officers in trouble. A National Guard troop on stand-by, fully geared, had marched in along with the agents and officers of multiple agencies and made a hundred arrests.

By the time it had all been sorted out, the hospitals had treated countless injuries, and many, like K.O.'s, although not life-threatening, were deemed war wounds by other officers, and harbingers of bleaker days.

K.O. nursed a black eye and a few bruised ribs. Breathing was painful, and laughing impossible. She doubted she'd have much to laugh about in the coming days.

Kepa Nahua had not been arrested for inciting a riot, and K.O. was crabby about that, too. The one bright spot in her day was her date with Alani that evening. They were to meet at the Oceanarium restaurant in Waikiki—one of her favorites because of the two-story, salt-water fish tank housing multitudes of gorgeous tropical fish.

The day passed slowly. K.O. rode the desk in Evidence, logging in countless bits and pieces, checking others back out again for court appearances. She supposed it was better than sitting at home doing nothing.

Rather than drive home over the Ko'olau mountains again, she had brought a change of clothes to work. She had comp time coming and had taken off half her shift. No one would have argued anyway with her elevated, "walking-wounded" status.

She showered and applied make-up in the women's locker room. By six she was ready in her short, black cocktail dress, and heavily made-up black eye.

Oh, well, she thought, taking a last look in the mirror. *At least I'm color-coordinated with my outfit.*

The sun was low on the horizon when she pulled into the hotel garage. She hurried through the carpeted lobby and saw Alani's handsome figure approaching from the opposite direction. They met at the restaurant's host podium.

The subdued lighting caused him to do a double take as he leaned in to kiss her hello. "Is that what I think it is?"

"If you think it's a hickey, then no." K.O. smiled. "A little souvenier from the demonstration."

Alani's lips tightened. She wasn't sure if it was because of her injury or her reference to the conflict.

"Never mind," she continued, "it's fine. Do we have reservations?"

Alani locked eyes with her a moment longer, and she felt he was saying he would allow her to table the topic for now. "Yes, we do."

The host returned from seating a large party and showed them to a table slightly elevated and back from the enormous fish tank. K.O. preferred this view, since she could see more of the wonderful specimens including a few small reef sharks.

"Wine?" Alani asked.

"Yes, thanks." K.O. suddenly felt nervous. She had already had several dates with Alani, in addition to their fire-filled initial relationship a number of years ago. *No reason to feel uncomfortable, right?* But K.O. did have a reason. The issue of race had intruded, and she wasn't sure how to deal with it.

Alani ordered wine and turned to look at her. His brown eyes seemed large, and the crests of his thick hair caught the light like sun on waves. He suddenly smiled and she felt enormously better. He reached over and took her hands. She cringed at her sweaty palms.

"Schoolgirl nerves?" he asked.

"Something like that." She smiled back, and the same old feelings hit her like a brick. The butterflies in her stomach started a chorus line, her heart pounded, and she felt warm.

Hot, in fact.

Alani lifted her hands to his lips and kissed them. The heat burst into a four-alarm fire and she leaned in and they kissed. Gently at first, but then more intensely. He was the first to pull away.

"Wow."

"Yeah. Wow." She was still sweaty. Well, maybe glowing by now, but for an entirely different reason. He still held her hands, and the roughness of his palms, hard and calloused from canoe paddling, felt unbearably sensual on her softer skin. She allowed her gaze to flow from his hands up to his shoulders where the material of his dress shirt pulled tightly against the muscles of his upper arms and torso.

"Here we are," cooed the wine steward. K.O. and Alani flew apart as if on springs. The bottle was shown to Alani, who nodded without looking at it. The wine duly sampled, poured and left on the table, the intruder left.

K.O. had regrouped by then. "So, how was your day? What did you do?"

"I sent off a shipment of *koa* bowls to the Mainland and got an order for three more. I have orders a month in advance—I'm swamped." Alani ran a hand through his wavy hair.

"Business is good?"

"Too good. I—" He was cut off as a waiter appeared.

"Ready to order?"

K.O. looked blank. She hadn't remembered menus on the table. "No, not just yet."

"Okay. Be back in a few." The waiter disappeared.

"I guess we should look?" K.O. made it a question.

"I'm not in a hurry. Are you?"

Her stomach flip-flopped again. She knew she couldn't eat a bite at this moment if her life depended on it. "No. I'm in no hurry."

His gaze swept her face, and she felt, as she always did, that he was seeing inside her. That he could, if he wanted, observe the blood racing in her veins, her cells moving about their work.

Unnerving, but she was getting used to it. On some level, she was comforted in knowing that although she might look horrible—as in her black eye—he didn't really see that, didn't judge her by appearance. There were times, however, when he looked at her and she was mesmerized by the desire in his face, the tension in his limbs. She felt herself mirror that same want.

"So, wanna talk about this?" His thumb grazed just below her rainbow eye.

So much for him not seeing it, she thought.

Not really. "I suppose so." K.O. sipped her wine. *Nice.* "What were you doing at the rally?"

Alani sipped his own wine and watched her over the rim of the glass. "I am Hawaiian, K.O. I have a stake in what has happened, and will happen to Hawai'i."

His comment about "the voice" came back to her. "You mentioned the 'voice of the people.' Did you mean, just in the Hawaiian sense, or in the organization?"

K.O. held her breath. The conversation had taken a turn and she couldn't stop herself from pursuing it. Important to know these things. If they were to have a future.

Future. What was she thinking now?

Alani's face hardened. "What's the difference? The organization is the people. No one will speak for us, and perhaps that is right. We need to speak for ourselves, for our rights. It's only a matter of time before the truth wins out."

K.O. had stepped in it. Their date had gone south. This side of Alani was new to her. She knew he loved his family—in fact they were her first "family" after she had arrived in Hawai'i from the Mainland so many years ago. She had become *hanai,* adopted, into the Okita *ohana,* and had been happy to stay there when she needed them. As she had come into her own, joining the police department after a series of apartments and dead-end jobs, she had weaned herself from them, although her best friend from the police academy, Lana, was Alani's little sister.

She had never sensed this . . . well . . . militant side before, in either Alani or in other family members. Now thinking on it, several of Alani's childhood friends were also musicians, and perfect recruits for an organization like *Ka Leo.*

Her head swirled as she struggled to quell her police instincts, even as her heart sank, knowing this could be the proverbial straw for the newborn camel that was their rekindled relationship.

"Alani," she said softly and laid her hand over his on the table. It felt hard and tense under her slim fingers. "Do we have to do this now?"

"No. I guess we don't." Alani still looked chiseled in the reflected light from the large fish tank. "It's going to come up sometime, you know that, K.O."

"I know. It's just now occurring to me that we might not be the same."

Alani barked out a short laugh. "Just noticing this, are you? You'll make detective yet."

"Very funny." She stroked his hand lightly and he turned it in hers so they were clasped. "I have never looked at you or your family as different from me, except in that external way, that we don't look the same." K.O. was suddenly uncomfortable. Voicing what seemed to be now naiveté, a complete disregard for his experience regarding race, made her squirm. She shook her head, thinking of all the hours she'd put in dealing with exactly this: race related crimes, disputes, slurs, you name it. How could she think she'd be immune in her personal life?

"What?" Alani asked at her head shake.

"I'm just an idiot, that's all." She smiled weakly. "What are we gonna do about this? You and me?"

Alani sipped more wine. "Have dinner?"

K.O. let it go. She really did want to have a nice dinner with this warm, wonderful, special man. The thought of Alani's head on her pillow again flashed through her.

"I do have to tell you, though," Alani flipped open the napkin covering the bread basket and offered her a piece, "that this is just the beginning for Hawai'i's people, not the end. I'm going to be there to show my support. Are you going to be there with me?"

Rats. A test question. She had automatically reached for a roll, which now sat like a hockey puck in her hand. The memory of the rally, her in uniform, Alani obviously in support of *Ka Leo,* flew to an image of her and Alani standing on opposite sides of Waimea Canyon—the Grand Canyon of the Pacific.

CHAPTER THIRTEEN

K.O. slept alone. Woke alone. Even Teresa had deserted her. She pulled on jeans and a T-shirt and puttered around the house. She even sat at the table and studied for the Sergeant's Exam. She was surprised to find she had retained much previous material. New concepts, however, flowed through her mind like the surf on a beach—laces of foam swirling and disappearing into the sand, never to be seen again.

K.O.'s thoughts swirled along with the seawater. Her date with Alani last night. Would they ever have a normal conversation?

"This is like the starving children in India syndrome," she complained to Teresa.

Teresa had been "helping" her study, her striped, tabby breast a millimeter away from the open book, *Management Strategies for Government Employees,* her paw occasionally swatting at turned pages. Many of the pages had claw marks, and the corners of several books had been chewed.

"You know, your mother tells you to eat all your vegetables because there are children starving in India?" Teresa didn't blink. "It's like that. I certainly can't change Hawai'i's past, and I may not even be able to help alter the future, but I'm feeling guilty because it all may cause me to lose a guy I like, who's not even my boyfriend. Kinda sorta." K.O. slammed the book shut, receiving stink eye from Teresa. She stroked the cat who raised her rump and waved her tail. "Yeah, well. I'm going nuts. I gotta get outta here."

K.O. locked up and drove to the station. At least she could do paperwork. However, first she had something on her own agenda.

When she arrived, she greeted the clerks and other officers before prepping her personal coffee pot with Kona Mac Nut coffee. While it brewed she pulled the phone to her and dialed.

"White Collar Crime. Aalu."

"Hi, this is Ogden in Evidence. I'm working on something and wondered if you had time to answer a few questions?" Not even a lie.

"Yeah, sure."

"What do you have on timeshare schemes on a place called Waikiki Tradewinds? They got a sheet, yet?"

"We watch all the timeshare deals pretty close, but we don't do anything unless we get a complaint."

"Anybody file, yet?"

"Try wait. I'll look." Computer keys tapping.

The coffee was done. K.O. took the receiver with her and added sweetener and half and half to her coffee, then sat back at her desk.

"Uh, oh."

"What, oh?"

"Flagged."

"What's that?"

"Open investigation. Plus a bunch of classified stuff."

"What's that mean?"

"Means it's flagged for one 'nother case that's also under investigation, and I don't have access to dat. Kinda weird, yeah?"

"Yeah. Weird. That happen often?"

"What?"

"That a case is flagged so you don't have access?"

"Hardly ever. Dat time Marcos came from the Phillipines and all the security was flagged, like dat. Oh, and den somebody was caught shoplifting shoes outta Liberty House. Walk right outta there in da shoes! I remember dat." The detective chuckled. "Flagged a shoplifting case. Fo' nothing, though, cause nobody press charges once dey found out was like one international incident. Cheez."

"Okay, so what you're telling me is Waikiki Tradewinds timeshares is already under investigation with you folks. Like what, bogus condos?" K.O. blew on her hot drink.

"Yeah. I don't have it all, not my case, but from here"—more keyboarding—"looks like we getting ready to indict. Which means, dey also might be getting ready to skip."

"Skip?"

"Yeah. Dese condo guys all foreign owners, practically, and dey smart. When dey know dey got all the scams dey can, outta there. Back home, whereevahs. Dey leave a nasty paper trail, make hard to track. Dey count on dat. By the time we catch up to dem, we been around da worl' six times already with banks and accounts and houses and shit. By den though, got a bunch a agencies in on it, international and all, and dey count on dat too. We all ovah asses and elbows, all filing papers and gettin' in each other's way. It's a mess."

"Sounds like a mess. Does it list the owner?"

"Nope. Tol' you. We got layers and layers, here."

"I might have something else. I got a business card that says Kepa Nahua, sales associate for those condos. He's the same guy who's president of the Hawaiian Cultural Society, right?"

"Dat *Ka Leo* guy?"

"Yup."

"Maybe da guys with dis case already know, but I'll pass it on. Dey not here, now or I woulda let you talk to dem. Save us all time."

"I figured. Can let me know if you hear anything, yeah, brah? I'd really appreciate it."

"Sure. Ogden, you said?"

"Yeah, K.O. in Evidence. Three to eleven, or you can page me. I'm also doing a bunch of Special Duty and security for the *Ka Leo* sovereignty thing, so I'm not always around. You in on that, too?"

"Nah. I got my hands full already."

"I guess. Thanks, eh, brah. Bye."

"Laters."

K.O. sat back and thought about her next step. Nothing to do about Richard and Abby yet, until she knew what was going on with Waikiki Tradewinds condos. Now that she knew it was *that* Kepa Nahua mixed up in it, her feeling of dread increased. She punched in Nahua's information on the computer and his sheet popped up.

She rocked back in her chair, eyes narrowed.

Just as she thought. Whole lotta speculation, but nothing serious. Arrests for illegal demonstrations, but no overt violence. Disturbing the peace. Public nuisance. Sealed juvenile record. She could get that if she needed it, but she would wait. Probably nothing serious anyway—pranks, toilet papering, stuff like that—but who knew for sure? He seemed slippery and smart. Too smart. Several arrests, no convictions.

Now this murder. Nahua proclaiming yet another slur on the Hawaiian Cultural Society by the U.S. Government, when the Lt. Governor's liaison had the nerve to turn up murdered.

She remembered the rally just before all hell had broken loose. Nahua bristling with self-righteous indignation, as if Larry Ellis had gotten himself murdered just to slow negotiations. Or the government had offed him for the same reason.

Jeez, now she was being stupid. What a mess. She rubbed her hands over her face, slapping it to get the circulation going and to snap herself out of that train of thought.

Selena, her chief clerk and good friend, stood before the desk. "Yo, boss, why don't you let me do that?"

K.O. looked up. "Very funny. What's up?"

"Kimo, I.D. tech from S.I.S., is here with evidence to log."

"Big deal. I got worse problems," K.O. grumbled and took a tepid sip of coffee, thereby furthering her crabby mood.

"This is from the leeward homicide. That Ellis guy from the Lt. Governor's office. Thought you'd want to see it personally, but if you don't . . . ." She turned away in a mock huff.

"Yeah, yeah! I'm coming." K.O. heaved herself from behind the desk. As she headed for the main counter, she put her mug in the microwave to reheat.

"Hey, K.O. Howzit?" Kimo from the Scientific Investigation Section—the crime lab—greeted her with a big smile and a wave.

"Good, Kimo. How you?" K.O. liked Kimo.

Small and dark, and rarely without a smile, Kimo was one of those people who would always look like a big kid. That he wore oversized Aloha shirts in deafening prints, surf jams to his knees and rubber slippers, didn't help him look any older. Probably in his late twenties or early thirties, his *hapa*-Hawaiian heritage ensured that he'd still be smooth-skinned with a full head of silver hair late in life.

"Got stuff for you." He thrust out several odd-shaped bags of varying sizes. K.O. read each inventory and checked that the items matched the description. Even dirt from the cave was included.

"What's this?" K.O. asked suspiciously of a desiccated brown-gray substance.

Kimo grinned. "Just like she says on da tag. Guano!"

"Crap?"

"Not just any crap. From da cave. Guano, crap, poop, sh—"

"All right, already. I get it," K.O. interrupted. "Why?"

"Donna say get everyt'ing, so I do. Everyt'ing." Kimo's brown face practically split in two.

"Cheez, Kimo, you gotta take her so literally? I better watch what I say to you."

Kimo laughed. "That'll be da day. I gotta go. Good to see you."

"Good to see you, too."

"Oh, by da way. How's da studying for da Sergeant's Exam going?"

"What, was it on the news or what? Everybody knows?"

"Nah. Just a few. But one of dem is me, so dat's just as good!"

"Get outta here, you." K.O. leaned over the counter, and they hugged. "Go!" She pushed him away, laughing.

"Nobody loves me," she heard him mutter as he walked slowly, body slumped nearly double, to the door. "I'm da best, you know."

Turning, Kimo looked serious. "No one's ever said dey couldn't make a case because I nevah collect all da evidence. No one's ever gonna say I missed something. I nevah heah you complaining when was your ass I was looking out for." The grin was back.

K.O. put out her hands in a defensive pose. "You're right, you win. I gotta talk to Donna, though, fo' reals. You need some reeling in, brah."

K.O. was still smiling as she placed the evidence in with the other homicides in the big room.

CHAPTER FOURTEEN

K.O. saw it in the *Honolulu Advertiser* the next day, just like everyone else. "ELLIS LINKED TO BIG BUSINESS LOBBY."

She read the article. "Larry Ellis, the representative in the Lt. Governor's office handling the negotiations between the Hawaiian Cultural Society and the Hawaiian government, was found murdered in a sacred Hawaiian burial cave on the leeward coast Monday.

"An anonymous tip led reporters to a paper trail, revealing that Ellis was behind big bucks supporting the golf course consortium that has been moving ahead with plans to evict one Hawaiian family (see accompanying story, EVICTION OF STEWARDS OF ANCESTRAL LANDS MOVES FORWARD, A3).

"The Lt. Governor's Office has released the following statement: 'We are concerned with the allegations surrounding Ellis's murder and activities linked to the golf course issue. We are determined to discover the truth.'"

"Ha! That's a load," K.O muttered. "And it means **exactly** nothing."

She turned to look at the companion article on A3. It was

about the Kanealiʻihiwi family's fight to remain on their homestead. It seemed the homestead had been deeded to the family generations ago by King Kamehameha, and was always to remain in the family's possession. Now the validity of that had come into question, and the eviction process had begun. The family was fighting it in court, but the legal fees were astronomical.

What a paradox. K.O. agreed that land should be preserved, left undeveloped, but at what cost to the people? She hated to see another shopping center or golf course go in as much as the next person, but what was the right thing to do?

She tossed the paper down in disgust.

She idly reread the evidence log, pausing as she came to Ellis's sheet. She popped up the homicide report on the computer and read that. The whole thing was a big mess, and getting messier. She was glad she wasn't in Homicide's shoes, but a feeling of dread tingled through her as she thought over the case.

At first glance, it was a dead guy in a cave. Not so different from any other murder. Then it was a prominent government figure. In a sacred Hawaiian burial site. Then the victim was white, and an integral part of very volatile political negotiations between the Kingdom of Hawaiʻi and the U.S. Government. Throw in the ramifications of defiling a sacred site, sprinkle with bribes and back-alley golf course manipulation—another sensitive, highly flammable subject in Paradise—and what did we find? A big, hairy mess.

K.O. sighed and ran her fingers through her hair. She was bothered on a number of levels, but the two that hit home hardest for her—aside from the wrangling that was becoming her Special Duty career as a riot-buster—were Alani and Richard and Abby.

Alani, because she truly didn't know if this could cause an irrevocable rift. Her job vs. his culture.

Abby and Richard, because it appeared they had been taken advantage of financially and emotionally, neither of which blows she thought they could afford. In addition, their "sales associate" was the head not only of a huge real estate scam, but of an organization with national and international ramifications.

"Argh!" Her first duty, she decided, was to protect Richard and Abby as best she could. Then she could sort out her feelings with Alani.

She pulled out the condo papers she'd obtained from Richard and perused them. They seemed legitimate, but she didn't know enough legalese to tell for sure.

She dialed her friend George, an ex-policeman turned lawyer, specializing in representation of police officers. He didn't pick up, so she left a message on his machine explaining her problem. "I'll drop the papers by your office and call you in a few days, okay? Take care."

That done, she turned her attention back to the Ellis homicide. It nagged at her, like the itch from a mosquito bite, and though she tried to distract herself with her own work and the stack of Sergeant's Exam materials, she couldn't help but scratch.

She pulled the phone to her once again to call her friend and nightclubbing buddy at the Medical Examiner's Office.

"Hey, Donna, it's K.O. Howzit?"

"Good. You?"

"Good, too. I got a problem with that Ellis homicide."

"Jeez, who doesn't? The M.E.'s leaning on me because it's so political. This case is really bugging me."

"Me, too. That's why I'm calling."

"Something doesn't sit right about it. Not my job, you know, but I can't get it out of my mind."

"Yeah. Not my job either, but I think I'm kind of in the middle of it somehow."

"Yeah? How?" K.O. heard Donna slurp something and remembered her own coffee, probably icy again by now, sitting in the microwave.

The women had been instant friends upon Donna's hire in the M.E.'s office. Few women were in police work or related fields, and K.O. often formed strong friendships with those who were.

She told Donna about the timeshare Abby and Richard had bought from Kepa Nehua.and her growing suspicions about his association with *Ka Leo* and its possible involvement in the Ellis murder.

For a few moments the phone was silent as each digested her thoughts.

"Well," Donna said at last, "I'll keep you posted as best I can. I first thought it had to be committed by a *haole* for him to be put in that cave, but now I'm not so sure. Talk about your double-blind, red herring, false trail, whatevers!"

"I know what you mean," K.O. agreed. "I thought the same thing. Something political to do with the *Ka Leo* negotiations and all that. Man, that line has sure blurred, hasn't it?"

"Yup. I can't tell who's on what side and for what ulterior motives. Every time something seems to make a little sense, a new puzzle piece goes missing."

"Now throw in that golf course thing. I can believe that. That means big money in this state. But trying to snag it from Hawaiian lands seems like suicide to me."

Donna snorted. "Total stupidity. It's not legal, is it?"

"I think it comes down to who's got the most money. I bet it's not that family on the land, or even the Hawaiian Cultural Society. I bet you anything it's some big group of lawyers out there funded by big time companies fo' days."

"This doesn't make sense, though. Okay, say Ellis worked for them or took money, whatevahs. Make him disappear, right? But they left him in that cave. For sure he was gonna get discovered." K.O. heard a big sigh. "This just makes my head hurt. It's not even my case until it comes to trial if I need to testify, but I can't leave it alone."

"I know what you mean. It's not *my* case at all, and I can't leave it alone. Thanks for talking to me. It makes my head hurt, too. Laters, girl."

"Yeah, K.O. Laters."

Her phone rang immediately. "Ogden. Evidence."

"Hi, K.O."

Alani.

"Hi, there. What are you up to?"

"Wanted to know if you're free for dinner?"

"Sure. What time and where?"

"My place. After you get off work. I know it'll be late, but I wanted to make you dinner."

Wow. A new and interesting development. She had never been to his place before, and he had never cooked for her. Maybe something exciting would happen tonight. A little spurt of adrenalin tickled in her belly.

"Sure. I can get off a little early and be there about eleven?"

"Great. When you get here, just come on in. I'll be slaving in the kitchen making you a fabulous meal." She heard the smile in his voice.

"Thanks. See you then."

"Bye, K.O."

Ooooh. There it was. That silky smooth way he said her name, like Kahlua and cream. *Yikes.*

"Bye." She hung up the phone with a hand that trembled slightly. The day was definitely looking up.

CHAPTER FIFTEEN

K.O. willed the day to pass quickly, logging evidence and playing phone tag. She selfishly prayed that nothing new would pop up that would interfere with her date with Alani.

She made herself study *Acme Metropolitan Policing for Lieutenants and Sergeants* for an hour at her five o'clock "lunch" as she hid in the Korean restaurant in the next block.

Her wish for no interference was granted, and she made it to Alani's condo, also on the windward side, just before eleven. The complex was sprawling, and following his directions in the dark was hard. She thought she had found the right section when the evening's rain began.

The windward side was lush and green because it rained nearly every day. The regular drenching made silver ribbon waterfalls against the emerald mountains, the foliage tall and sweet, and mud for days. It also made finding one's way in an unfamiliar condo complex even more difficult.

The rain fell in great sheets. obscuring the numbers on the buildings. It also made K.O. extremely cranky, since she knew her dressy blouse and black pants would be soaked. An umbrella didn't help much when it rained sideways. The wind whipped fiercely, and the only advantage tonight was that the clouds scudded quickly across the moon, allowing bright if intermittent light. In one such gap she saw the building she'd been seeking. Her Parking Fairy worked her magic—a guest space appeared directly in front.

Things were looking up.

She bundled up as best she could against the storm and bolted for Alani's front door. She knocked, but after a moment with no answer, she decided Alani couldn't hear over the storm. And, after all, he had said just to come in.

She entered a foyer with soothing pale tiles extending throughout the house as far as she could see. A large ti plant sat in one of Alani's beautiful pots.

He claimed he was a carver by trade, making his living creating exquisite works—bowls, stands, frames, and figures in a variety of woods. He had recently begun to toy with clay, however, and as in all the other avenues of his artistic expression she had seen, he had produced wonderful pieces. Some functional, like the pot in the entry, and some merely beautiful, begging to be picked up or stroked.

She slipped off her pumps, adding them to the footwear lining the shoe rack. In Hawai'i, no one wore shoes indoors at home. You could always tell a good Hawaiian party by the number of shoes left on the front porch, she mused as she wandered down the hall.

She carried a bottle of wine and her dripping coat, not wanting to leave it in the hall. She faintly heard the rain as it whooshed outside. As she was about to call out, she heard Alani's deep rumble over the sound.

She followed his voice and, instead of finding him in the kitchen, tracked him down the hall to a door left ajar. She saw a wedge of carpet and figured *bedroom*. She was about to knock, and make a joke about finding him in the bedroom upon her arrival, when the tone of his voice stilled her hand.

"Brah, I am doing everything in my power to make this thing

come off. I have as much at stake as you do." A pause. "No one
was supposed to get killed!" Another pause. "I don't like it. We
knew the risks were great, the cost might be high, but—"

K.O. shifted miserably in the hallway. She was suddenly not
only wet, but enveloped in an icy chill.

What to do?

"Kepa, look. I said I'd help, and I will. I am. But, man, *Ka Leo*
is getting so radical. Can't you do anything?"

Well, that answered her question about who Alani was speaking
to. Kepa and *Ka Leo* all in the same minute.

K.O.'s stomach rolled. She would not have been able to eat
anything now if someone paid her.

"I gotta go. I'm expecting someone."

Great. Not a date, not a girlfriend, just "someone."

Tears prickled her eyes. She felt angry and used. Angry at Alani
and the tears.

Just what was going on here? She didn't want to be caught
listening at doors, but she had to know.

Two could play this game. She had been played, so she would
play back.

K.O. retraced her steps. As she reached the foyer, she heard
Alani close the door. She was so upset her hands shook. She threw
her still-dripping raincoat over the shoe rack, not caring now if
the water shrank his leather loafers to the size of soap dishes.

"Hi!" Alani said, stepping towards her.

Startled, she forgot the wine bottle she still held. It slithered
through her wet hands and shattered on the tile. Chardonnay
splashed up her pants. It missed Alani entirely, but she got a grim
satisfaction from the sight of the rapidly spreading lake.

She had been genuinely surprised at dropping the wine, and
hoped that would cover any unusual expression she still wore. Alani
hustled off and returned with several towels. He blotted the floor
while she stood unmoving and mute. By the time he finished, she
had recovered enough to stammer out an apology that nearly

choked her.

"That's okay, K.O. I'm just glad you made it here safely in the rain."

"Me, too."

"Do you need to rinse out your pants right away? It looks like an awful lot of wine is on there. I have some sweat pants you can borrow until they dry."

"That's okay, really," she managed. "I think it's mostly rain."

He led her through the house to the kitchen and small dining area, which looked out onto a patio. He was solicitous and friendly, warmth emanating from him. Nowhere could she detect the steely voice she had just heard him use on the phone.

He guided her to the table, which was set with flowers. A card with her name on it sat on one of two woven placemats.

"I have to do a few things, but have a glass of wine." He poured from an open bottle on the table and went around the divider to the kitchen to open the oven.

He was still talking, but K.O. had stopped listening.

She opened the card. Stars, planets, and moons decorated the front. "May all your nights be filled with joy and may all the planets move in harmony with us," he had written in his bold script.

Half an hour ago, this would have filled her with unbridled joy. Now she felt nauseated. She wanted to run. How could she have been taken in like this? Was she that smitten that all of her cop instincts had been dulled? She had to say something.

"Alani? What's happening with the Hawaiian Cultural Society stuff? What are you working on with them?" Smooth move Ogden. Interrogation 101 was paying off. She felt disjointed and unable to create a better opening.

Alani didn't seem phased, however.

"Mostly I'm helping with fundraising. You know, that family they're trying to evict? You know—the Hawaiian Homelands one? The HCS is helping with the legal fees. I'm organizing some things for that."

I just bet, K.O. thought bitterly. Alani set a large *koa* bowl filled with salad in front of her, along with another filled with Hawaiian sweet bread rolls he had just taken from the oven.

"Go ahead, dig in. The pasta will be ready soon." He poured a glass of wine for himself, and when K.O. didn't move, served her some salad. "Papaya dressing. That's okay, isn't it?"

"Sure. That's fine."

He looked at her oddly, but K.O. couldn't summon the energy even to fake interest. "So, I'm organizing one of the Thomas Square Craft Shows as a benefit for the family. All the artisans have agreed to give a percentage of their profits that day to offset legal costs. We're having *huli-huli* chicken, *kal bi* beef, you know?"

K.O.'s mind flew to the Hawaiian quilt on her bed. Handmade, and purchased from a Thomas Square Craft Show. She remembered walking through the aisles of many booths. Vendors, selling all manner of Hawaiian crafts, pottery, carving, jewelry, clothing. She had happily wandered the fair, the sun beating comfortingly on her head, the barbeque smells pungent and rich, until she'd rounded the giant banyan tree in the middle of the park.

She'd had to give the tree a wide berth because it was huge— many feet across and taller than some of the surrounding structures—with hundreds of ropelike vines dangling from its branches. At least twenty-five children had hung like a band of chimps, climbing, swinging, laughing and shouting. She had just reached the back side of the tree, narrowly missing a tiny Tarzan, when she had spied the quilt, hanging from a rack. The brilliant colors and painstakingly stitched flowers had beckoned to her. At first glance the price had made her gasp, but she had eventually given in and had never regretted it.

Now, sitting at Alani's table, listening to him go on about the fundraiser, she wondered if she'd ever be able to bring herself to return to a Thomas Square Craft Fair.

"K.O. What's the matter? You look strange. Are you sick?"

Once again, K.O. was struck by a paradox. Alani had always

been caring and loving towards her. When she had been injured on a previous case, he had literally flown to be by her side. If she hadn't heard him on the phone just now herself, she would never have believed it. Her earlier determination to accuse him, accost him, pry out the truth had drained away along with the blast of adrenaline and her appetite.

"Yes. I do feel a little sick. Maybe I should go." She looked across the table at him and saw only warm brown eyes, filled with concern. No mention of how much time and effort he must have put in on this dinner.

She hardened her resolve. What was a little effort at a dinner to have a cop on your side? To have a source of inside information? She had never revealed active case information to anyone not directly assigned to a case, but this battle between the U.S. Government and the Hawaiian nation was a completely different animal. She was in it up to her neck. Every cop on the force was. And, now, it appeared that Alani was, too.

The tears came back.

"K.O., you are sick. Why don't you sleep here tonight?"

"No!"

He looked surprised. Her heart wrenched with such pain it made her gasp. She had had every intention of sleeping here tonight if all the years of waiting for him had pointed her there. To have it offered—after her discovery of his betrayal, and under the guise of illness, not romance or love—was beyond enduring. She staggered to her feet. "I just need to go home."

"Okay, let me help you. Are you sure you can drive?"

"Yes." *Please don't touch me, please don't touch me. I couldn't bear it if you touched me right now.* He must have sensed her withdrawal because he only followed her down the hall and held her coat out, not offering to help her into it. She snatched it from him, making sure her hand didn't touch his, and bolted into the storm.

She drove home too fast, the pounding rain on the windshield competing with her tears in destroying her vision.

At home she tore off her clothes and pulled on sweats and a tee, before falling into bed in the dark. How had everything that had seemed so right gone so terribly wrong so fast?

She was still awake, although exhausted and depleted when the day dawned.

She vowed she would shut herself off from these emotions from now on. She would not give him her power. She would do whatever she needed to see that this case proceeded with all her cooperation—all personal feelings aside.

Now, all she had to do was believe it.

CHAPTER SIXTEEN

The day began gray and dreary and did not improve. That was fine with K.O. She dozed off and on all morning, Teresa stationed on the pillow next to hers. The rain beat down, not soothingly, but harshly, violently at times, bending the red ginger and heliconia double with its force. Her periods of sleep were not restful, filled with images and shadows. Each time she woke she felt disoriented and more exhausted. Finally at noon she gave up, rose for the day, and made coffee. Even her favorite flavor, Mac Nut Fudge, didn't pick up her spirits. The idea of food turned her stomach.

She debated calling in sick. That was certainly true enough. She still felt ill.

In the end, she decided to go into the station early. She dragged on a uniform and drove over the Pali for her third-watch shift. She would not let Alani win even this tiny victory of making her miss any work.

At least there was no shortage of work to occupy her. In her office, pink message slips were piled in the middle of her blotter, weighted down by a plastic-wrapped chocolate chip cookie. Homemade by the looks of it.

Selena popped her head in. "Hey, boss. Made cookies last night in a fit of PMS. Saved you one." Then she got a good look at K.O. who still stood by the desk, purse, jacket and files in hand. "What's up? You look like shit."

K.O. threw her coat over the back of her office chair and dropped her purse into the large desk drawer. "I feel like shit." She sat slowly, gingerly, as if sitting too hard would cause something to break. Maybe it would. She carefully moved the messages and cookie and set the files on the desk.

"What's wrong? Didn't you have a date with Alani?"

K.O. nodded.

"Woo hoo! Good for you!" Then Selena caught her bleak expression. "Oh . . . sorry. Didn't go well, I take it?"

"It didn't go at all. I don't want to talk about it." K.O. ran both hands through her hair and sat with her head in her palms.

"Sure. No problem. Let me know if you need anything."

"Thanks . . . . Selena? If anyone asks, I'm not here yet, okay? Some things I need to do."

"Yeah, sure." Selena quietly closed the door.

K.O. sat for many long moments, unmoving, before she picked up the phone and dialed Homicide, eventually reaching the person she wanted.

"Roly. It's K.O. in Evidence. Howzit?"

"Good. What's up?"

"You know the Ellis murder? I have some stuff on that through the timeshare condo thing that Kepa Nahua's been doing."

"Yeah, what?"

"This is tough. Let me begin at the beginning, okay?"

She heard the small detective's chair squeak as he shifted. "You bet. Shoot, K.O."

K.O. had first met Roly on a series of homicides a while back. She had been in the Records & ID Department then, and the police department had still been housed in the old Sears building. Roly had been newly transferred to Homicide at the main station and had helped her on another case. She had always found him to be a good listener, patient, kind, and—best of all—a solid detective.

K.O. started with Abby and Richard, and the timeshare they had bought. She added the Special Duty assignment at the Shell, remembering vividly the toppled amp and the bright blood of the mother.

She moved on to her run in with Blala and what Sam the water vendor had told her about *Ka Leo* working under the guise of the Hawaiian Cultural Society.

"Yeah, we know about those things. And thanks for the tip on the timeshare. Nahua's greasy prints are all over this case—these cases. I hope we have enough paper to write it all up. I want to get that bastard."

K.O. had rarely heard Roly swear. It took a lot to rile him up. "I wanted to give you the background because I may have something new."

"Go ahead."

K.O. took a deep breath, then expelled it. Her left leg began to twitch, and she absently massaged it. "I have a new lead on someone who may be involved in Ellis's murder."

"Who?"

"Alani Okita."

There. She had said it. Done her duty. She felt as if she might throw up.

"What do you have?"

"I overheard a conversation connecting him to Kepa Nahua and *Ka Leo,* as well as at least some knowledge of the Ellis murder."

"He look good for it?"

"No! I mean, I don't think he committed it. But accessory either before or after is possible." K.O. heard her heart begin to crumble, bit by bit. "He's close to Nahua, and has a working knowledge of the HCS and by extension *Ka Leo.*"

"Um, hmmmm. I don't have his name here. He new with the organization?"

"I don't think so, but I don't know. I think he keeps a pretty low profile." The understatement of the year.

Roly asked more detailed questions about Alani, and with every answer, K.O. felt herself growing a little more numb. By the time she hung up, she felt she was a ball of ice ready to shatter.

She was surprised to note that her shift had begun and the office had not changed, the world had not ended. The pink messages still sat on the desk, weighted by the cookie.

Jerking to her feet, she grabbed her purse and coat and left the building by the public entrance to walk quickly up Beretania Street. The sun had come out a bit, and although the day was still chilly, it was much warmer than K.O. felt. She strode blindly along, past the small graveyard tucked between buildings near Ward Avenue. She glanced over the wall at the sad little markers, listing and moldy, scattered underneath the shedding plumeria trees.

Without thinking, she crossed Ward and headed straight into Thomas Square.

Silent now. No craft fair. Too cold for the average park-goer, the block-square park was bleak and lonely. She approached the old banyan tree and sat on a wet bench nearby, feeling the damp rush through her pantlegs and skin to meet the ice in her veins. The vacant park had a derelict air, depressed and run-down.

She sat in the cold vacuum and heard children laughing as they swung on the vines, saw again the bright colors of her quilt as if for the first time, and smelled sweet Malolo juice intermingled with smoking briquettes.

CHAPTER SEVENTEEN

When K.O. returned to her office, she determined to lose no more professional time to personal matters. She hardened her heart and efficiently logged evidence, reviewed and wrote reports. She spent an hour on the Sergeant's Exam study materials, and noted with cold satisfaction that she felt ready and focused for the test next week. Apparently the months of study, alternating with days of learning by osmosis, had paid off. Nothing and no one was going to stop her from passing that test and getting stripes and a Sergeant's position. It was one thing to pass the test but another to receive a decent assignment.

As she neared the end of her shift, she realized two things. One, that she had not eaten all day. Even the cookie still sat on her desk guarding its pink charges. Two, she had not dropped off the timeshare-condo papers to her lawyer friend George.

Dammit. Too wrapped up in myself. Feeling sorry for myself, she thought as she stuffed the manila envelope with the condo contracts into her purse. She checked out of the station a little early, taking her dinner break as the last hour.

Only ten o'clock. She could drop the papers by George's office through the mail slot. As she drove towards his small office, she had a sudden change of heart. What she really wanted to do was see George in person. He would listen, talk, entertain—and he usually stayed up until all hours.

She headed towards George's small, but adorable house on the side of Punchbowl, a long dead volcanic crater, smaller than Diamond Head, which housed the National Memorial Cemetery of the Pacific. The site was set smack in the middle of a residential area, ringed by houses of all sizes and designs, which clung to the slopes.

She parked along skinny, one-and-a-half lane Puowaina Drive and descended a steep, narrow cement stairway to the front door.

She always marveled how folks could get all their furnishings up and down these steps. Since a good portion of the island of O'ahu was made up of mountains and valleys, many of the homes were built on precarious perches or tucked into cliff sides, making access and parking difficult. In addition, with housing so expensive, much of it was rental, and moving households a common occurrence. K.O. herself had moved a number of times when younger, living in the communities of Manoa, Pauoa, Mililani, Waikiki, Waipahu, and even, briefly the posh district of Kahala, all in just a few years.

George's house had a small front yard, but stood "backwards" on the lot as far as K.O. was concerned. Its front door faced the crater and the road, and the back of the house would have had a magnificent ocean view, had there not been a jungle.

She saw lights on inside and pushed the bell. She heard it jangle distantly and saw a shadowy figure approach.

George opened the door, registering at first surprise, and then delight.

"Scarlet! What are you doing here?"

"Hi, Rhett. Came to pay a social call." She returned his banter in her best—or worst—Southern accent.

He wrapped her in a big hug. He had been her Field Training Lieutenant a hundred years ago, and although she had been so much younger than he, a different gender, and far below in rank, they had become friends. He had begun calling her Scarlet because she wore lipstick. In retaliation, she had called him Rhett. There had never been anything romantic between them, just some common ground and respect.

He had retired a few years ago and put himself through law school, wanting to help police officers in trouble. K.O. could not think of a better man to do it. Now he had a small but thriving practice, and they rarely talked, much less saw each other. In the way of old friends, however, they picked up right where they had left off.

He ushered her inside—his tall, well-built frame still firm from daily jogging—and guided her to a comfortable couch. Then he sat in a ratty recliner where he had obviously been working.

Papers and files littered the floor and nearby furniture, but K.O. knew they would all be organized and in precisely the right order.

Light glinted off his silver hair, a little thinner now, as he smiled warmly at her.

"Can I get you anything? Coffee? Wine?"

"Glass of wine would be good." K.O. noticed a highball glass on the end table. "What are you having?"

"Bourbon and Coke."

"Got any more?"

"Do I remember correctly, bourbon and something diet?" He said the last like "arsenic?"

K.O. laughed. "Yes, diet if you have it."

George shook his head glumly and rose, crossing the small room to a brightly lit kitchen nook. "You know, it's just sad the way some people never change."

"Yeah, I know what you mean," called K.O. She glanced around the room noting police photos, guy-bonding pictures of various camp outs, fishing trips, etc. A floor-to-ceiling bookshelf covered the far wall, and she examined its contents. A great many law books, but also a wide range of other material, including mystery, science fiction and "literary fiction," as well as some interesting coffee table books.

George returned with her drink and a bowl of macadamia nuts. "I am so addicted to these," he said, as he put them down.

"Me, too. I'll just save you from them." K.O. helped herself to a generous handful.

"So, my dear, what brings you to my door in the dark of night?"

"Did you get the message I left about the timeshare condo thing?"

"In fact, I did. There's a lot of timeshare scamming going around. You know real estate law isn't my area?"

"Yes, but I don't know too many lawyers, and even fewer I'd trust with my mother's best bridge buddies. I'd never hear the end of it if something happened to them. It'd be all my fault, no matter what. You know that."

George nodded soberly, remembering the one time he had met K.O.'s parents on a visit from their home in Seattle. K.O. had been held responsible for everything from the weather to the food.

"Why don't you fill me in?"

K.O. did, as they sipped drinks and the mac nuts disappeared. She handed him the papers, and he perused them silently, the only sound in the room the flipping of pages and the clink of ice, as it melted and shifted in their glasses.

George handed her back the papers with a sigh. "They look legitimate. Full of crap the average person wouldn't notice, but airtight as far as I can tell." At K.O.'s bleak expression he added. "I'm sorry, honey. It's what these guys do. They have a platoon of lawyers for just this reason."

He returned to the kitchen with their glasses and brought them back full. K.O. was about to object but then thought, *What the hell. I don't have to drive home tonight.*

She took a big slug and felt it burn all the way down. This drink was stronger than the last. George must have figured she'd need it. He was right.

George pulled some papers towards him, set his glasses back on his nose, and began to read.

K.O. sat and mulled. What should be her next step? Follow up with the detectives in Homicide and White Collar Crime. She knew Kepa Nahua was up to his eyeballs in both areas, and neither were her concern, except that Abby and Richard were being taken to the cleaners.

Alani popped into her brain and she took a big swig of bourbon, hoping to dislodge him. Tears came, and she furiously swiped them away, telling herself it was the strong drink. How could she have been so wrong? About a man she had known for years? Granted, a several-year hiatus was part of the equation, but did people change that much?

Here she sat, on one side of a huge gulf of Hawaiian history and culture, with Alani on the other. That was bad enough. Now it looked as if he was involved in a homicide.

Could that ever be justified enough for her to look beyond it to the man, and not just as far as the act?

Another horrible thought occurred. What if Alani were not only involved in that, but in everything? Maybe he was even higher up in the *Ka Leo* organization than she knew? *I didn't even know he was involved in the sovereignty issue—even periferally—until this week!* she thought. Maybe he was involved with more than just fundraising.

Her head swirled. What if everything she had thought about him was not real, but only her fantasy?

She moaned, and suddenly felt George's arms go around her, pulling her to him. He sat with her in silence while disjointed thoughts filled with self-doubt and self-loathing rocketed around her brain.

Sometime later, he tucked her in on the couch, swaddling her with a knitted afghan. Eyes closed, she heard the click of the lamp turning off and the pad of his feet as he went to his own room.

Blissfully, she was too drained to torture herself further with Alani or Nahua, or even Richard and Abby, and she drifted off into a dead sleep of shifting shadows.

CHAPTER EIGHTEEN

K.O. woke with bright morning sun streaming in and wondered for a moment where she was. The couch she rested on was comfortable and unfamiliar. Although disoriented, she wasn't worried. She smelled coffee and buttery toast and sat up, stretching. The evening came back to her, but without the intensity or power of last night.

Thank you, George, she said silently. She didn't have more than a mild headache—much less than she deserved after two strong drinks and nothing to eat but nuts.

She padded to the bathroom. Then, much relieved, she wandered into the kitchen nook and found George reading the paper, a pile of buttered toast, a glass of juice, and a cup of steaming coffee in the empty place across the table from him.

"Morning, Sunshine," he said.

"Morning." K.O. sat down and doctored her coffee with sweetener and half and half, and took a grateful sip. Next she slugged half her orange juice and felt her depleted cells positively plump right up. She smiled.

"Better?" George inquired.

"Much." K.O. grabbed a piece of toast. "Thanks for last night."

"You're welcome. I'm only sorry I couldn't offer better news."

"Me, too. But, at least, now I know. Besides, you've worked your magic. I don't feel so despairing about it, even though nothing's really changed."

"You might want to hold off on that. Here, look at this."

"What?"

George handed her the front page of the *Advertiser* and she read the headline. LOCAL SLACK-KEY ARTIST FOUND MURDERED—SUSPECT IN CUSTODY.

She read the story. "Oh, no. Oh, no."

"It gets better. Did you see who they suspect murdered Blala Richards?"

"Oh, God. It's my fault. Alani." The pit dropped out of K.O.'s stomach. "That can't be right. I can't believe it. This is all my fault!" Her hands trembled, rattling the paper.

"How is this your fault, honey?" George's voice was gentle as he pulled the paper from her clammy hands.

"I told Homicide about Alani. They would never have arrested him if I hadn't done that." She inhaled shakily. "I don't know. I was mad at him, and I told myself I was only doing my job. But he didn't do it. I know he didn't. I couldn't be that wrong!"

"K.O., no one wants to believe the worst of someone she loves."

"Love?" K.O. interrupted. "This isn't about love, George. This is about a crime and justice." She told him about the dinner at Alani's house, and the conversation she'd overheard.

When she finished, George just sat and stared at her silently.

"Do you think I may have overreacted to it a teensy bit?"

"Who, you?" George snorted. "Let your emotions get the better of you? Nah. You're superwoman."

"All right, already. Shut up. Maybe, just maybe I should have thought a little first. And now they've arrested an innocent man because of me!

"You don't know that. You don't know what they found—the circumstances of the crime; the evidence."

K.O. gulped her coffee. "You're right about that." She straightened her spine. "I'm going to find out exactly what's going on. You can bet on that. I do know they wouldn't have arrested Alani without my pointing a neon sign at him, complete with road map."

"Honey, you can't even be sure about that. He could have been found standing over the body with a smoking gun in his hand, and nothing you said or didn't say would have affected that."

She was about to make a sharp retort, when she realized, just maybe, he was right. She bit back her words, knowing her old friend was just trying to help. In fact, maybe he had helped by focusing her on the facts, not her own assumptions.

"Okay. Even if he was found with a smoking gun, there is an explanation for it that will clear him of murder, and I'm going to make sure that happens. I had a hand in doing this, and I'm going to have a hand in undoing it."

"You should have become a lawyer." He smiled. "Remind me to call you if I ever get in trouble. You sure stick by your friends."

"You do, too. Thanks, George. I'm going to get going. I've got to clean up and get to the station. Uh, oh."

"What's wrong now?"

"Teresa's probably royally pissed I didn't come home last night."

"I didn't know you had a roommate. And why would she be mad? You're a grown up."

"Not a roommate. Worse. A cat."

"Ah. That is a serious matter. Animal neglect is a serious crime. I suppose she'll be contacting me and I'll get a fat retainer."

"You'll get a fat lip, Rhett Butler, if you ever take my cat's case over mine!" K.O. stood and went around the table. She hugged him tight and kissed his cheek.

"Yes, ma'am. Call me if you need anything."

"I will. You can count on it. Don't get up. I'll let myself out. You've really helped me. You always do."

K.O. gathered her purse from the living room, folded the afghan, and let herself out into the cool morning.

CHAPTER NINETEEN

K.O. left the quiet coolness of Punchbowl and hopped on the nearby Pali Highway to reach the windward side. As lush foliage whipped by, she registered its beauty automatically, passing the exit for the lookout and zipping through the tunnels with only minimal attention.

She pushed and pulled the bits of the case around in her mind. They felt like pieces from several different puzzles. She listed the things she knew. Kepa Nahua, president of the legitimate Hawaiian Cultural Society, and reputed leader of the radical *Ka Leo O Kanaka*. The HCS, ostensibly for promotion of Hawaiian Culture here in the islands and around the world, versus *Ka Leo,* a rapidly surfacing underground movement to send Hawai'i back to the age of the monarchy. K.O. knew she was simplifying the issues but brushed away those thoughts as her mind pressed forward.

Larry Ellis, the Lt. Governor's liaison to the Kingdom of Hawai'i negotiations, now linked to extortion in a golf course consortium determined to snap up Hawaiian land, and in particular, a nice parcel of Hawaiian Homelands. The distinction was not lost on K.O.

Hawaiian soil was precious in that not much of it was available and useable. Much was mountainous, and unbuildable, never mind golf-able. That left already developed land—not much of that for sale; land used by the U.S. Government for military bases and training grounds—lots of that; and Hawaiian Homelands—land set aside years ago by monarchs for the perpetual use of the Hawaiian people. A small percentage of land was privately owned and could probably be bought for the right price.

Ellis had been murdered and left in a Hawaiian burial site. Someone was mocking Hawaiian customs and culture, if in fact he had been placed there with knowledge of their sacred beliefs. That piece of information stood out in K.O.'s mind. The awareness of what that act meant to the Hawaiian people pointed to motive. If, in fact, the victim had been placed there with that knowledge, it was an intentional slap in the face of the Hawaiian people.

Would a true Hawaiian do that? She didn't know. Would Alani? She really didn't know.

Fear trickled down her spine at how much she didn't know about him. Was he capable of murder? She knew he believed in the Hawaiian people, past, present, and future with all his heart and soul. What was he capable of? That was the question.

Which also begged the question of price. Anything could be bought for the right price, her jaded history in her chosen profession reminded her. K.O.'s mind jumped to the family stewarding the Hawaiian lands and facing eviction. How was such a thing even possible? If King Kamehameha, or whoever, had granted those lands more than a hundred years ago, how could they be taken away? She didn't know.

Kepa Nahua was also involved in an internationally owned corporation buying and selling timeshare condos. That went back to owning versus leasing land and condos or houses, which in Hawai'i was not the same thing at all.

K.O. had shopped long and hard for a condo that was fee simple, as opposed to lease hold. In a lease-hold condo or home, the building might be yours, but the land it sat on wasn't. Owners of the dwellings paid rent to the owner of the land. It made for interesting evictions—having to remove your whole house if the owner of the land booted you off.

K.O.'s friends on the Big Island had had to move their house off lease-hold land and rebuild it on a new parcel. Fortunately, Hawaiian hearts are generous and they'd had tons of friends to help with the mammoth project. K.O. shuddered to think how many innocent foreigners or Mainlanders bought a home, not realizing they didn't own the land beneath it.

Many of the hundred-year-old leases were coming due, and owners were putting their houses on the market in hopes of selling before having to do something dire. There was no guarantee that a lease would be renewed. If a lease was renewed, it most certainly wouldn't be at the same rate as instituted in 1900.

Now she knew Alani was linked to Kepa Nahua in some way. It couldn't be good, any way she looked at it. All her questions seemed to be answered the same way: *I don't know.*

This morning's paper had added another piece to the puzzle she was having trouble picturing. Blala Richards's murder. It made no sense to her at all, but she refused to believe it was unrelated to the Ellis case and the other things involving Kepa Nahua. The word "coincidence" was not used much in her line of work.

Blala was supposed to be Kepa Nahua's right-hand man. For years, he had been a star in the local slack-key galaxy, and K.O. confessed to having at least one of his cassettes. She would miss his contribution to Hawaiian music.

He had also been active in the Hawaiian Cultural Society, a beloved Ambassador of Hawai'i at world-wide concerts, even appearing in famine fundraisers and disaster-relief concerts. Up until she had literally run into him at the Shell, she had only seen the jolly, laughing-musician persona he portrayed publicly. She had never seen or experienced the mana, and, if not hatred, then disdain he held for non-Hawaiians.

"Just goes to show," she grumbled. "You think you know

somebody—" she cut herself off because Blala Richards had become Alani in her mind and once again she felt duped.

Maybe Richards was murdered because somebody wanted to make a point. But who? That seemed pretty farfetched.

Maybe he was murdered because he was no longer useful as Nahua's second in command. Maybe Alani now held that post.

Hardly realizing it, she had arrived home, showered, and changed, all on auto-pilot. She focused as Teresa's strident wailing made it through her foggy brain.

"Sorry, sorry." K.O. picked up her cat's solid, grey-striped body and stroked her. Teresa quivered with righteous indignation. Her food and water bowls were empty, and she had made a political statement next to her odorous litter box.

"Teresa, I've been a bad mother. Okay, okay." She corrected all her errors, even bribing Teresa with small balls of cheddar, a favorite treat, which she gently rolled across the tile. Somewhat mollified, but still refusing to forgive completely, Teresa allowed K.O. to cuddle her in the recliner that faced the lanai and emerald Ko'olau mountains.

As K.O. let her thoughts drift with the clouds, a rumbling purr under her hand suggested she might be forgiven soon. She felt her tension ebb a little, and faced what she had denied for so long.

Alani was caught in the middle of some huge wheel, and now she was there, too. For as she continued to pet Teresa and watch the clouds form and dissipate over the cardboard-looking ridge, she admitted she was in love with Alani, and despite the way things appeared, she would help him.

CHAPTER TWENTY

After so long denying her feelings for Alani, the admission came as somewhat of a relief. It galvanized K.O. into action.

She set Teresa in the recliner, bid her good-day, and shot out the front door, prepared to do battle with HPD or whomever to free Alani.

She spent the drive back over the Pali girding her loins, planning impassioned speeches for his release, and—only half-joking—plotting escape schemes.

All for naught. She arrived at the station, hackles raised, to find Alani had been bailed out.

"When? By whom?" she demanded of the uniform at the receiving desk.

"A couple hours after he was arrested. By his sister." The officer turned away, obviously finished providing information.

K.O. turned away also, brain humming. Alani's sister Lana was a police officer, and one of K.O.'s best friends. Lana had married Lance Chang, a deputy D.A., a few months ago. K.O. had attended the ceremony, and that event had been instrumental in rekindling her romance with Alani.

Well, at least Alani has good people on his side.

Without realizing it, K.O. had wandered up to her office in Evidence. She sat at her desk and dialed Alani's home number.

No answer. She dialed Lana's.

"Hello?"

"Hey, Lana. It's K.O. Howzit?"

"Not so good. You heard about Alani?"

"Yeah. That's why I'm calling. Is he there?"

"Yeah. Hang on." A clunk as the phone was set down, murmurs and footsteps. The phone was picked up.

"Hello?"

"Hi, Alani. How are you?"

"Compared to what?" The old joke surprised K.O.

"You sound pretty good, considering."

"Considering I was arrested for the murder of a friend and then publicly humiliated? And, incidentally, I'm innocent, not to mention saddened by that loss."

"Richards was a friend of yours?" *Jeez, will wonders never cease?*

"Of course. We worked together with HCS. He did valuable work for our cause."

And scared the crap outta me, but I'm sure he was a lovely man.

"Can I see you? I need to talk to you."

"Sure, K.O. I have things I want to tell you, too." His voice had that buttery-soft quality that made her knees turn to water.

She shored up her weakened resolve. "So, where and when?"

"I have to meet with my attorney at three, but I'm free until then. Magic Island?"

Magic Island. Not an island at all, just a spit of land, a bulge of beach, with an enchanting name, and even more enchanting memories.

"Sure. Half hour?"

"See you then."

K.O. hung up and pulled the Evidence log to her. She watched the entries swim and dance before her eyes, making no sense of them, as she was swept back in time to Magic Island.

A date with Alani. One of their earliest, but one of the most romantic. He had picked her up in his old truck, and they'd had an early evening picnic, walking the warm sand, watching the beach-goers pack up, and the die-hard surfers challenge the waves and tides of the Ala Moana boat channel in the setting sun.

They'd talked and held hands, kissed and hugged. They'd sat in the back of the pick up, watching the moon rise, turning the black sea into crests of mother-of-pearl. Sipping a bottle of wine, talking of dreams, a future. Their kisses and touches growing more urgent, more fire-filled. They'd finished in the bed of the truck, secluded by palms and rocks at the far point of the "island," a private place, a sanctuary in safety and love.

Even now, sitting at her desk, K.O. smelled the sea, heard the waves and the creaking of nearby moored boats, felt his strong hands running down her hips. She shivered and stood, suddenly needing to be at Magic Island, to see him there again, even though the circumstances were completely different, the hopes and dreams of that night shattered in the reality of this time and place.

K.O. knew Alani meant that same spot at Magic Island, so she parked her silver Crown Vic and walked to the point where the rock piles faced the sea. She sat on a sun-warmed boulder and waited.

He approached noiselessly, and even with her heightened senses, she neither heard nor saw him, but felt him. He stood behind her and placed his rough brown hands on her shoulders, the comforting weight and warmth making her close her eyes and just absorb him.

She opened her eyes when he gently kissed her cheek. "Hey," he said softly. He sat next to her on the large rock, their thighs only inches apart.

"Hey, yourself," she said, pulling herself together. *It would be so easy to get lost in him again. I could just let go and drift.*

His brown eyes studied her, his full lips wore a half smile.

"What happened, Alani?" She meant it to sound interrogatory, but it came out plaintive.

"I don't know." He looked out to sea. Was he lying, avoiding her gaze?

K.O. decided to take a harder line. Even if she loved him—maybe especially because she loved him—she had to know what was going on if she was going to help. Even if it cost her the relationship.

"Start with the night of our dinner date and go on from there."

Alani glanced back at her, lips pursed. She'd seen that look a million times during interviews. He was gauging how much to tell her. He sighed.

"After you left, I couldn't sleep. I was worried about you. You seemed so . . . upset."

"I was sick, remember?"

"Yes, but there was something else."

K.O. definitely did not want to get into that. She didn't want him to know she'd overheard his phone conversation. Not yet.

"So then what?"

"I did some work and eventually fell asleep in the studio."

She knew he used his garage as his wood-working space. She nodded.

"The next day I had some meetings and paperwork and—"

"What meetings? With Richards?"

Alani shifted on the boulder. "Well . . . yes. And with some other people from the Hawaiian Cultural Society."

"What kind of meeting?"

"Fundraising, things like that. The rally coming up and the plans for Aloha Week." He again watched the ocean.

"Alani. Look at me." He did. "Everyone knows that HCS works with *Ka Leo.*" She refrained from using the much stronger phrase "is a front for." "I know Richards worked for both organizations and that he was considered the muscle, practically a hit man for them." She shivered again at the memory of Richards's massive shape blocking her physically and mentally at the concert. "I need to know, Alani. Do you work for both organizations, too?"

His bronze skin went sallow. He licked his lips, but held her gaze. "If you had asked me that a week ago, I would have said no. But now, I don't know anymore, K.O. Something's changed. Even when I was at those meetings, it seemed like they were discussing things underneath what they were really talking about, you know?"

K.O. nodded, but didn't speak. She wanted to keep him talking.

"I felt like I was watching a tennis match, and somehow, I was in the middle, but never knew it before. It sure feels like that now. Richards and Nahua, and a couple others really got into it over what I thought was something small, but they were so . . . intense."

"About what?"

Alani took her hand and held it. It felt cold to K.O. "They were talking about publicity. It appeared to be about the Aloha Week publicity, but now I think the undercurrent was something more. I don't know what. I can't pinpoint it. Kepa wanted more, really over the top and over budget, since Aloha Week is all about things Hawaiian anyway, and Richards was digging in his heels saying 'we did enough, already,' which was kind of unusual, since he always seemed to go along with whatever Kepa wanted. It's just a confusing jumble in my mind, now."

"Okay, it'll come. Then what?"

"I went home after the meeting, not really even thinking about it much. I have a new order I'm working on, and a big set of *koa* bowls for a Mainland store, so my head was really on wood. I worked super late and was so tired. When I cut my hand on the chisel, I decided to quit for the night. I slept in the studio again, and HPD woke me up banging on the door. They arrested me for Richards's murder. I was covered in sawdust and dirt, still in the clothes I slept in, with blood on my hands. Of course it was my blood, but it didn't look good."

"So you have no alibi, no witnesses, nothing?"

"Nope. Lana and Lance bailed me out and got me a great lawyer, but man, I'm scared."

K.O. studied his profile. His copper skin was still pale and his hands around hers were clammy.

"I will help you, Alani, but you have to promise me something."

"What?" His eyes held hers.

"I can only help you as a police officer or as a friend, but not both. I am both, but that's not going to serve either of us. I'm going to proceed with this like it's my case, as a police officer. I already know things that make this look bad for you, and more will come out." K.O. felt a twinge of guilt about the phone call, and how she'd told HPD about it, but not told Alani.

Alani nodded. "I understand."

No, I don't think you do. Not yet. She hoped he never would find out that she'd told Roly about the phone call. "So, the promise is, that no matter what happens, no matter how bad things get, know that I am doing this for you. Because I care about you." She couldn't bring herself to say "love."

"I know."

"I hope so. Because if you did commit murder, I'm going to find out." Alani opened his mouth as if to protest. She plunged ahead. "And if you didn't do it, I'm going to find that out, too, and make sure everyone knows it."

"K.O. I didn't do it." This time she avoided his gaze.

"Okay. Who did? You must have some idea. Nahua?"

"Jeez, K.O. I just don't know. If you'd have asked me even a few months ago if Kepa could have done it, I'd have said no way. But now I don't know."

"Yeah, well, Homicide thinks *you* did. They're happy with you as their suspect, and they may not look for evidence that clears you, only evidence that supports them. And when they get enough, all the bail money in the world isn't going to get you out."

"Oh, God." He tightened his grip on her hand.

"And another thing." When Alani faced her this time, his eyes were rimmed with tears.

"What now?"

"If you didn't do it—" she held up her hand like a stop sign to forestall his words—"and I don't know what evidence they have against you yet—you should watch yourself."

She barely stopped herself from telling him it was Kepa Nahua, in her estimation. If Alani was conspiring with Nahua, or even worked for him in some way, she would only alert him that she knew. She loved Alani, but she couldn't trust him.

What a pretty picture, she thought. Rock-solid foundation for a relationship.

She knew herself well enough to understand that matters of the heart required extra care. And in this case, might get her killed. Even for love, that was a risk she would not take. Yet.

CHAPTER TWENTY-ONE

After K.O. and Alani had parted at Magic Island, K.O. felt at a loss as to how she should proceed. She ended up back at the station, in front of Roly's desk in Homicide.

After she told him she was sorry she'd given him the tip about Alani, he showed a tendency to clam up. "Come Roly, give me a break. What's going on?" K.O. had a cup of nasty Homicide Division coffee cooling on the desk in front of her. Why did Homicide's coffee taste so much worse than everybody else's?

Detective Rolipsky, slight of build and dapper of dress, rocked and squeaked his chair annoyingly as he studied her. She wanted to grab him by his perfect lapels and shake him, screaming, "Stop it! Hold still, dammit!" But she held her tongue, hoping for information she had no right to.

"K.O., we appreciate the tip on Okita, and he looks good for it. What else do you want me to say? Now you're telling me he didn't do it, couldn't do it, blah, blah, blah. He was covered with blood—"

"Covered? How covered?"

"Dried blood on his hands, and lots of it."

"Didn't it test out to be his?"

"Yeah, so what? Richards was stabbed to death with a wood-working chisel, found at the scene. Matches the tools in Okita's workshop."

K.O.'s heart skipped a beat. Alani hadn't told her Richards had been stabbed. And with a wood-carving tool. "Didn't Alani tell you he'd cut himself working?"

"Yup. Wouldn't you? He's careful. He was really careful not to get Richards's blood on him, but just in case, he cut himself afterwards, so we'd have to find the exact spot to test."

"That sounds a little far-fetched to me."

"Yeah, it would. You know, K.O., we don't solve the majority of cases—only a few. We only catch the dumb crooks. Lots of crooks are smart, really smart. Alani is smart. We sealed his workshop, took all the tools and stuff he was working on for evidence. You'll see it soon enough."

K.O.'s stomach lurched at how the investigation was zeroing in on Alani. Impounding all his tools and pieces also put his career at risk. She knew many of his tools were one of a kind, or gifts given by other artists—irreplaceable. Of course, he could buy tools in the meantime, but who knew how expensive that would be? And his work! Her heart was heavy at the idea of his beautiful wood stashed in the impersonal evidence room. And for how long? He said he was working on two new orders—big ones it sounded like. She scrubbed her face with her hands in frustration.

"Shit, Roly, that's his work, his bread. He can get tools, I guess, but can't you guys rush the tests on the wood pieces and release them so he can at least earn a living?"

Roly looked as if he was about to protest with the standard "lab tests take time and nothing can be done about it" line, but something in her face made him stop.

"K.O., you ask a lot. I'll call Kimo and ask. That's the best I can do. I know we won't release the tool with the blood on it, or anything else that shows blood or fibers, but if—and it's a big IF—the rest is clean, I'll see if I can get it all released. But it won't be for at least a couple weeks, that I know. I'll do my best, and only for you."

"Thanks, Roly. You won't be sorry. I'm not saying he's not involved with Nahua, but I'm sure he didn't have anything to do with Richards's murder."

"You better be right about that." Roly went back to squeaking the chair. "Well?"

"Aren't you going to call Kimo at SIS?"

"Shit, K.O., you don't want much, do you? The lab works when it works, and pissing them off isn't going to make it happen any faster."

K.O. clasped her hands together under her chin and made puppy-dog eyes.

"Christ. Fine." He explained quickly to Kimo what she wanted, grunting several times in response. Then he thrust the phone at K.O. "Wants to talk to you."

"Hey, Kimo, howzit?"

"Whatchu doing, girl? You think you the only case in town, or what?"

"Kimo, you're the best. I need you. Can help me or what?" She kept her voice matter of fact, avoiding Roly's glare.

Kimo's voice softened. "Course I will. I do what I can, okay? I cannot release anyt'ing with blood or li' dat, but I work hard on the other stuffs so he can work, 'kay den?"

"No ka oi, Kimo, you know that? You da bes' brah. I owe you, and you remember that." K.O. lightened her tone. "Plate lunch a week for the rest of your life?"

"And dats jus' fo' starters," Kimo's elfin chuckle crossed the wire and she felt him smiling.

"Take care, Kimo. Talk soon, eh?"

"Fo' sure. Laters." K.O. hung up and looked at Roly, who still glared at her.

"What? I get you a plate lunch too, brah. No worries."

"I got plenny worries. If you're right, and I guess I hope you are, that means I gotta start all over again, looking for a suspect. And I still got the Ellis murder open." He sighed and pushed back from his desk, eliciting one last hellacious squeak from the chair.

"Cheez, Roly, you like get that fixed or what?"

Roly shrugged.

K.O. assumed a haughty, very bad, British accent. "I will give you the benefit of my pearls of wisdom, completely free of charge and unsolicited."

Roly laughed and stood, pulling on a light raincoat. "What?"

"You find Richards's murderer and you'll also find Ellis's, as well as the answers to a whole bunch of mysteries of the universe!"

"Gee, K.O. thank you. You really should put in for Homicide. I don't know how we've gotten this far without you."

K.O. laughed and pushed him towards the door.

They parted at the elevator. K.O. retrieved her car and decided it was time to see her friend Donna Costello at the M. E.'s Office. She felt better than she had in days.

CHAPTER TWENTY-TWO

K.O. pressed the buzzer outside the Honolulu Medical Examiner's office. When Donna's terse "Yes?" crackled through the intercom, K.O. answered.

"Hey, seestah! It's K.O. Let me in! Let me in!" She heard Donna's laugh and the door latch released. K.O. made a dive for the knob. The heavy door released a wave of frigid, slightly chemical air that settled over her and reminded her what lay behind the downstairs doors.

She quickly headed upstairs to the offices. At the top, her friend Donna waited smiling.

They hugged hard. Although they didn't see each other often, cases did bring them together occasionally. And, if Donna was present, someone was dead, so their meetings were not usually pleasant.

The last one had been a freeway jumper that had slowed traffic on the H-1 for miles, but their favorite one to rehash was a murder where a man had poisoned his wife.

The case had been a mess. The woman had called her daughter on the Mainland to tell her she thought her husband—the daughter's step-father—was poisoning her. She left a frantic message. The daughter was not at home so she returned the call the next morning. The husband answered and claimed his wife was drunk. The daughter, who knew her mother didn't drink, could hear her mother calling for help in the background. She told her step-father to call 911. He refused. The daughter hung up and called 911 from the Mainland.

The responding ambulance crew checked her mother and found pulse and respiration normal. They believed the husband's claims that she was ill, but would be fine. Several hours later, he called 911 to say his wife had stopped breathing. She was taken to the hospital and was in a coma for five days before dying.

K.O. and her partner were called to the hospital to take a report from the daughter, who had flown to Honolulu to be with her mother. K.O. and her partner believed the daughter and suspected the husband of murder. Donna came onto the case at the time of autopsy, which revealed deep tissue bruising, proving the woman had been strangled. K.O. tried to give the case to Homicide, who originally had said they didn't have any evidence of murder, or—at that time—even attempted murder.

When Donna presented them with evidence, they said that since K.O. and her partner had done all the work, they might as well finish the case. Donna told K.O. that the husband had called her to ask if she had discovered his wife had been strangled!

Unbelieveable, but true.

K.O. and Donna had worked long hours for many days to collect evidence that would stand up in court, and to build a solid case.

Donna guided K.O. to her office, and they sat on opposite sides of Donna's paper and "thing" covered desk. K.O. eyed a small bone weighting down some paperwork.

"What's new?" Each time K.O. visited Donna at work, she was shown some new and interesting piece of a case. Sometimes it was messy, but Donna's specialty was bones, the older the better, so often it was neat and tidy.

This time, Donna pulled a box from under her desk and said, "I have the most interesting case, but no idea what to do with it." She opened the box and revealed several human skulls and bits of bone.

"You are not going to believe this, but I got a call from a family that found this in their parents' things."

At K.O.'s questioning look, Donna continued. "The parents died—old, you know—and the kids were going through the house, cleaning and stuff, and found this box in the closet. Turns out they knew about the box for years, more or less, but didn't know what it was. Parents told them never go in the closet or something bad going to happen. So they didn't, until the folks died."

"Who's in the box?" K.O. asked.

"This is where the story gets weird." Donna smiled because K.O.'s face clearly showed that it was plenty weird already.

"We don't know whose bones are in here. I started doing some research on things the kids told me, and found out they belong to some Philippino religion, really obscure, that believes that raiding graveyards on certain nights, and keeping the bones secret, brings luck and power to the keeper."

"No shit!" K.O. had never heard of this before.

"Weird, yeah? So, anyway, the family luck would all run out if the kids found the box, so the parents made 'em all scared of the closet. The bones are all mixed and most of them are super old."

"Homicide? Like Frankenstein?"

"No. We don't think they killed anybody. Everything I've been able to find out, which isn't much, says they have to already be dead and buried and you gotta dig 'em up and save 'em."

"That is so sad," K.O. said.

"I know. I don't know how we're gonna inform families, or re-inter them or what." She smoothed the flaps back over the fragile contents and carefully put the box back under her desk. "So, that's one of my cases, anyway. I bet I know what you're here for."

"Hi, Donna. What's up?" said a voice from the doorway.

"Hey, Tiny. Remember K.O.?"

"Yeah. Hi, K.O." Tiny Sugano, Donna's investigator-in-training came in and shook K.O.'s hand.

"Hey, Tiny. Howzit?" K.O. didn't know Tiny well since he hadn't been working for Donna long, but she liked him. He always seemed helpful and his large frame, although solid, was graceful. She found him extremely useful on cases where strength or size was needed.

"So, what's up, Tiny?" Donna asked.

"Just filing some reports and thought I'd check in—see if you needed anything."

"Tiny is the worst report-writer in the world!" They both laughed. "So, he tries to make up for it by getting me coffee, playing secretary, and generally staying on my good side."

"So, you need anything?" Tiny leaned on the doorframe, arms folded.

"K.O., you want coffee?" Donna asked.

"Sure, why not? This might take a while."

"Thanks, Tiny," Donna said. "Grab one for yourself and join us because you know about this case, too."

Tiny shrugged and disappeared.

K.O. sighed and leaned back in the uncomfortable office chair. "This is driving me nuts, Donna. I want to ask you about the death scenes." When Donna didn't react, she added, "Unofficially, of course."

"Sure, K.O. No prob. But I'm getting lotta pressure from da boss because they're so political. First the Ellis guy, then Richards. But I'll tell you something—thanks, Tiny." Tiny had returned balancing three cups of coffee and dragging another chair which he set in the main doorway of her cramped office.

"Tiny was at both death scenes, too, so he can toss in his two cents." Donna lowered her voice to a whisper. "One guy did both homicides. I'd bet the farm on it."

"I don't know if I agree, Donna," said Tiny. "Both were so

different."

"I know. Supposed to look that way. I talked to Roly in Homicide and he agrees. We've looked at this thing six ways from Sunday, and it's something pretty big, I think."

K.O. nodded. "I think so, too. I don't know what exactly is going on, but I'm going to find out."

Tiny shifted his big body in the chair. "So, K.O., you working these homicides?"

"No, but I seem to be involved already. Some friends of mine are somehow connected—victimized, framed—I don't know." Her voice rose in frustration as she flashed to Alani at Magic Island. Even as she had pledged to help him, she had withheld something critical from him, and thereby risked losing him forever. Heaviness filled her, and then the frail, kind faces of Richard and Abby swooped in to make her misery complete.

Donna, noticing the melancholy, said in a falsely exuberant game-show-host way, "Okay, let's compare these crime scenes!"

That popped K.O. out of her reverie. Even Tiny smiled a little and shifted his chair to see Donna's computer screen.

Donna's sophisticated computer program brought up the cave scene photos, one at a time. She could split the screen with many small photos, show her notes, the reports, any variety of combinations to help record-keeping and investigation. They watched in near silence, Donna occasionally making an observation, or K.O. asking to see something again or in greater detail.

The cave was dark outside the ring lit by camera flash. The body curled in its niche, very little blood showing. Close-ups of the feet, hands, head, torso. The body out of the niche, same pattern of close-ups.

Other than the usual waxy look of death, Ellis seemed relaxed, his last moments not those of sheer terror.

Then they switched to Richards's crime scene. K.O. had not been there, but she had been to a number of murder scenes. This, however, was surprisingly graphic, and she felt moved because she had recently seen the victim alive. Most of the time, she did not know the victim, which made it easier to distance herself from the case.

Richards had been killed in his Kinau Street apartment, a warren of rooms under a house. The kitchen window actually opened into the garage, and the bedroom window, high above average window height, looked onto the street at pedestrian foot level.

Multiple stab wounds were the cause of death. As Donna put it, "He was more holes than body." In her estimation, the scene was meant to look like a home invasion, but the number and violence of the wounds suggested a crime of passion. Planned or unplanned was unclear at the moment.

Furniture had been tipped or ripped. Drawers rifled. Wallet and money gone. A few wall-hooks left naked, suggesting something had hung there. Art . . . photos . . . .

"Well, you know," Tiny began, "he was a big guy. Maybe it was a robbery, but 'cause he fought or was surprised, the assailant, uh, panicked?"

"Come on, Tiny. No way!" K.O. laughed. "Look at the scene, man. It's amateur. We're supposed to think it's a burglary gone bad or something, but it's clearly personal. At least that's what I get from it."

"Whaddya mean?" He sounded a little belligerent.

"Look at the violence of the death itself. Blood everywhere, even places you wouldn't expect it necessarily. Look at the spatter on the walls and how far it goes from the entryway and onto the carpet. Also, photos and knick knacks, art pieces have been thrown around and displaced. A burglar doesn't need to throw pictures around to steal stuff. I've been to lots of burglaries. They go for the places people hide stuff, like dresser drawers and under beds."

"What about wall safes and things? Don't people hide safes behind pictures?" Tiny asked.

"Well, yeah. But usually it's something bigger than an eight by ten!" K.O. and Donna shared a laugh.

"Seriously, though," continued K.O., "Richards's personal stuff, his art and photos, were moved, stolen or defaced. That's personal."

Donna nodded her agreement. "No worries, Tiny. You haven't been with us that long. You'll get the hang of it."

Tiny didn't look happy at having the two women discard his theory so quickly.

Donna and K.O. flipped back and forth between the two scenes. Easy to do with great software. Ellis had been shot. Richards was stabbed. They made notes, compared details, tossed out ideas.

"My head is spinning," K.O. complained. "I need a Diet Pepsi."

"Hey, Tiny, can you . . ." Donna began, but Tiny was no longer sitting in his chair. "Wonder when he left? I get so involved I forget to eat, much less pay attention to coming and going of the help!" She chuckled and stretched. "I got soda in the fridge."

At K.O.'s look she smiled. "Not that fridge." She stood. "Come we get a soda."

"Thanks. You've been such a big help, Donna." They walked down the hall to the lab. "The only thing I'm sure of is that both homicides were personal. I mean, Ellis, a *haole,* left in a sacred cave? Come on."

"I know. But I'm also sure the same person did 'em both." She forestalled K.O.'s question with a hand. "I don't know how I know it. I just do. I submitted all the evidence I had, and I'll check with the other shifts to see if they found anything else. However—and this is the main problem I have—they were such different people, with such different interests. Other than the fact that they are connected by that 'personal murder' bit, I don't see how they are connected. I mean, they're on *opposite* sides of the same issue. I guess we might be looking at two different suspects, but that doesn't feel right."

"I know what you mean. I so agree." They had reached the fridge in the empty lab.

"It's buggin' the crap outta me."

Donna opened the refrigerator. K.O. stared. It was full of baggies and petrie dishes and tubes and all manner of unappetizing things. Scattered among them were brown bag lunches, complete with names, several bottles of salad dressings, mayonnaise, pickles, and cans of soda and juice.

"What's your pleasure?" Donna's eyes sparkled at K.O.'s discomfort.

"Uh. Nevermind. I'm not that thirsty."

Donna laughed outright. "You'll never make it, girl! But I love you anyway."

K.O. laughed weakly at her own wimpiness. Well, *really*. Anything could have crawled up on one of those cans and . . . .

Donna was saying something K.O. had missed, ". . . so I'll call you if anything comes up, okay?"

"Absolutely. Thank you again. Just like that last case, we're not gonna let that bastard win, right?"

"Right!" They hugged tightly once again.

"I'll let myself out. You get back to your . . . uh, lunch?"

Donna chuckled again as she pulled out a canned juice. "You make me laugh, K.O. And that's not something I do very much around here. Take care."

K.O. slowly went down the steps to the main door, realizing as she stepped out into the heat of Iwilei, that she had completely gotten used to the smell of death.

CHAPTER TWENTY-THREE

K.O. returned to the station and eyed the ever-growing stack of pink message slips on her desk. Someone had appropriated the cookie. *Damn.* Wasn't that just the way?

She was about to cover the slips with a report and pretend she hadn't seen them, when the top name caught her eye. *Abby.* Not too many Abbys would be calling. The message had been left yesterday.

"Why didn't she call me at home?" K.O. wondered. She read the body of the message. Abby and Richard had called an attorney about the timeshare. Oh, boy.

K.O. immediately dialed. "Hi, Richard. It's K.O. Abby left a message for me about the lawyer? What's up?

Richard sounded exhausted. K.O.'s spirits sank even further as Richard relayed the upshot of the meeting. It had cost them $380 for the attorney to tell them what George had told her for free. The contract looked solid, and there was no way to prove they hadn't known what they were signing. Of course, they could go to court for how many more dollars, but K.O. didn't think either of her elderly charges were up to a lengthy court battle.

Guilt coursed through her because she had not called them

immediately with the results of her chat with George. Maybe she could have saved them some time and money—if not the stress.

"What's next for you two, Richard?" K.O. asked. Her brain ticked furiously, realizing the only way they would get any recourse at all would be if she could help bring down the Waikiki Tradewinds timeshare scheme. She slapped herself on the forehead with the audacity of that idea. If all of White Collar Crimes and how many other agencies hadn't been able to nail them, how could she?

"Golly, Katrina, we really don't know. We put most of our savings into this little nest in Paradise. Of course, we still have our house in Washington, but we'd really hoped to spend a lot of time here."

He sounded so beaten, her heart just clenched. "Where's Abby?" Usually, any phone conversations involved them both, a tag-team effort on two extensions. A bit unnerving if one wasn't used to it.

"She's not feeling well. This has really hit her hard."

K.O. instantly was angry all over again. Richard had the health problems. Abby was old and frail, but in pretty good physical health. All they needed was this blow to send one over the edge, and they both would spiral down.

"What do you kids need, Richard? I'll bring it right over. How about shopping? Do you folks need groceries?" K.O. knew they had a kitchenette in their hotel room and could make snacks and small meals. "Let's have dinner together, okay? I have a break later."

At Richard's hesitation, K.O. added, "My treat." He never passed up a free meal.

"I don't know, honey. How about if we call you later after Abby wakes up?"

Wakes up? "Richard, do me a favor, okay? Peek in on Abby and see if she's comfortable. If she's awake, ask her what she'd like me to bring her. I'll be over later even if we decide not to go out." K.O. was really worried. Abby never napped and, birdlike as she was, she needed all her meals.

"Hold on."

The phone thumped down and a vacuum of silence ensued. While K.O. waited she pawed through the first few message slips. Alani had called. Donna yesterday. She tossed that one. Tiny Sugano earlier; right after she'd left the Medical Examiner's Office, in fact. *Hmmm*. Strange, but maybe Donna had a new development.

"Katrina?" Richard was back. "Abby says you can bring her some of that Aloha iced tea she likes. The stuff in the can?"

A wave of relief washed over K.O. She hadn't realized how thoroughly prepared she'd been to hear Richard's panicked plea for help with his ailing wife. "Okee doke. You got it. I'll call before I come. If you think of anything else, you call me at the station, okay?"

"Sure thing, Katrina. Thank you." All the bluster was gone from his voice. As annoying and pompous as he could be, she missed it. It was part of him. All she could offer was damage control now.

After she hung up, she decided to start digging. Really digging.

She reread the newspaper articles on Richards's and Ellis's murders, then the accompanying article on the Hawaiian Homelands family eviction.

A photo caught her eye. It showed the extended family in front of their plantation-style home. A small, square Hawaiian house with slightly peaked roof and a raised, wrap-around porch sat amid lush banana trees, a patch of lawn, and the mountains rising sharply behind.

The article told more about the family than the political situation, but did touch on the fact that the lands were in jeopardy and could be up for public sale. A golf-course consortium (thus far unnamed) was pushing some legal loophole to forward the sale. The first step would be to evict the family, saying they were living rent-free and if they wished to continue tenancy, they would have to come up with market-value rent each month. The amount was ridiculous. The article added that taxes on the house had not been paid, and that was grounds for the consortium to start proceedings, once the property was in jeopardy. K.O. didn't know if that could actually happen, but it certainly was making a mess and shooting the family into legal hell.

Nothing new, but K.O. added the article and photo to her growing file of notes, reports, ideas, and increasing speculation. The picture of the stone-faced group haunted her, and she thought again of Alani's huge and loving family.

Today's paper had yet another article on Kepa Nahua and the Hawaiian Cultural Society—how he was misunderstood, that his actions had only to do with furthering the awareness of Hawaiian Culture—and that *Ka Leo* was far removed from his hand.

"Ha." K.O. tossed the paper, nearly crumpling it in disgust. Then she thought better of it and dutifully cut out that article, too. What bothered her most was his adamant stance that he had nothing to do with the murders—*well, duh, he would say that*—but that it was a government plot to discredit his organization. He still had not been arrested on any charges whatsoever. That really pissed her off. She immediately called her first-choice target.

"Roly. K.O. How come Kepa Nahua never get arrested fo' anything?"

"Hi, to you, too. What do you mean?"

"You guys arrested Alani, but never arrested Nahua."

"Chill, K.O. We had evidence, remember?"

"Yeah, I remember." *Thanks to me.* "But you gotta have something on Nahua. Even to slow him down a little!" she wailed into the phone.

"Man, K.O. my ear!"

"Sorry, eh?"

"Listen, just to shut you up. I been checking into what you said. Alani still looks good for it, but at least I got the investigation open to other angles, 'kay?"

K.O. was silent, pondering. "'Kay. But, I know Nahua is behind all this. I want to help."

"Yeah, you wanna clear your boyfriend is all."

"Roly. That's below the belt. When did I ever put my personal life ahead of an investigation? And I had plenny chances, too, brah. Besides, he's not my boyfriend. He's a friend I care a lot about."

"Yeah, big difference. Whatevers. Look, K.O., all I'm saying is, I'm trying. I'm working on it, and I'm keeping an open mind."

"But how can there be nothing on Nahua? Doesn't that even show you he's dirty?"

"Or innocent."

"No way. You're just not trying."

The huge silence that met this remark told K.O. she'd let her temper and her feelings push her way over the line. "Roly, I'm sorry. That was stupid to say, and I know it's not true." Nothing. "Really. I'm sorry. That was rude. Here, you just trying to help me and I get all *huhu* about it."

"I hate redheads."

K.O. knew she was forgiven. "Nah, Roly. You love us. We make the world an exciting place."

"You make my world a pain in da ass, girl." A heavy sigh. "Shit. Okay. I can't move on Nahua because we tryin' to nail him on a couple things. We want da stuffs dat will keep him in prison da longest. We have open cases all ovah on him and nobody wants to mess it up. So, shaddup already about Nahua. He's going down for something, but I don't know just what yet."

"I think—"

"Right now, I don't care what you think. Did it ever occur to you, you doin' the same t'ing to Nahua that you said we're doing to your not-boyfriend? That maybe he didn't kill these guys? Or even order them as hits?"

K.O. had no answer to that. It was true. Nahua was guilty of something—under investigation, but not necessarily for murder. Much as she wanted him to swing for those homicides, she had to consider that maybe it was just because she didn't want Alani to. Maybe she had to apply to herself what she had begged Roly to. If Alani didn't do it, and Nahua didn't do it, then she had to open her eyes to the possibility of a new suspect.

"Shit. Roly, you're right. I was doing exactly what I accused you of."

Roly sounded smug. "You sure did. Ha. How does it feel?"

"Like I really am ready to put in for Homicide."

Roly's belly laugh rolled through the phone. "You are so funny, K.O. That'll be the day!"

K.O. laughed, too, but it occurred to her that someday she might want to work in Homicide.

Not a bad gig, she thought as she opened her file again and began to sort her notes for the zillionth time. *Detective Ogden. I could live with that.*

CHAPTER TWENTY-FOUR

At the ME's office, Donna Costello was also going over her case notes. Everything added up wrong, no matter what she did. She checked the reports against the crime scenes. She compared her reports with Tiny's. Everything seemed okay, but she knew it wasn't. Frustrated, she called up the police reports, the evidence, and the crime scenes, and began anew.

"Hey, Boss. Howzit?" Tiny leaned into Donna's office.

"Not so good, brah. I goin' crazy with these two stupid cases. I'm missing something and I hate that." Donna sat back and stretched cramped muscles.

"Why don't you leave it alone? It's not like you don't have enough other cases."

"I can't leave it alone. I'm the only one who thinks the two crimes were done by the same guy. Even Roly is just humoring me. Ah, shit, I don't know."

"Maybe you're right."

"You think so? Why you say that? All along you been on the side of two murderers."

"Like you said, you missing something. You find it, you find da guy, yeah?" Tiny's white smile split his dark face.

"Yeah. You right, though. I got plenny cases I should be working on. Not losing sleep on dis one, eh?"

Donna slapped her folders shut with finality and moved them to an already piled-up corner of the desk. Then she closed out those windows on her computer and opened up the file on an ancient, emaciated woman who'd been found lying curled in the fetal position in her walk-in. She was ninety years old and weighed seventy pounds—suspected elder abuse by the adult daughter she lived with, who supposedly cared for her.

"Now, this is a case I can process," she said grimly.

Tiny nodded. "Yeah, it's better to close out the cases we can, instead of wasting our time on the ones we can't."

"Wasting?" Tiny was gone from the doorway. "Trying to do my job is not wasting time," Donna grumbled to empty air. "I going to have a talk with that boy," she added as she confirmed her notes and began the process to initiate a criminal case.

* * *

K.O. jiggled her leg impatiently in her booth at King's Coffee Shop in Kaimuki. Alani had agreed to meet her.

Well, agreed reluctantly. Refused at first, in fact.

Now he was late. *Okay,* not late, but in another minute, he would be late.

"Hi." Alani slid into the booth opposite K.O.

Startled, she jumped. She'd been so busy working up a good head of steam, she'd missed his entrance.

The waitress appeared instantly and set a glass of water in front of Alani. K.O. had been there five minutes and had not been approached. Another reason to be mad at him.

"What can I get you?" The waitress, young and buxom, clearly admired Alani's firm physique.

"I'd like some water, too," K.O. said more sharply than she'd intended. The waitress noticed her . . . sort of.

"Sure. Anything to eat?" Her attention was back on Alani, who obviously enjoyed it, along with K.O.'s increasing crabbiness.

"I'll have the Portuguese sausage and eggs, please," Alani said, adding a sparkling smile.

K.O. seethed. *"I'll* have the mushroom and cheddar omelette."

"Hon"—to Alani—"do you want rice or toast with that?"

"Rice, please." He made a point of noticing her nametag perched on her chest. "Cherry."

"Sure, thing." She smiled and collected his menu. She turned to K.O. "You?"

"Toast."

Huge sigh. "Okay." Cherry flipped up K.O.'s menu and headed for the kitchen.

K.O. gave Alani major stink-eye, but he just laughed outright, not hiding his enjoyment.

She decided not to let him stay so content at her expense. "Why couldn't you meet me?"

"I did meet you. See, I'm here."

"No, you said you couldn't. What was so important that you couldn't meet me to talk about your case?"

"I promised to help the Kanealiʻihiwi family today. I wasn't sure I could make it out to the homestead if I met you first. I called and said I might be late."

"This is important, Alani. It could affect your future."

"I know, but that is also important. It affects Hawaiʻi's future."

K.O. regrouped. She remembered the Kanealiʻihiwi family were the stewards of the lands who were facing eviction. She could not butt heads with him regarding things Hawaiian. A lose-lose situation, no matter what her personal opinion. "Okay. So you'll go late. I'm sure they'll be fine 'til you get there."

Alani's brown eyes hardened. "You just don't get it, do you K.O.? Not only might these people lose their home, but something larger is at stake. These lands were handed down by the king. They are supposed to be protected."

He studied her face. She didn't like the scrutiny. It made her feel small and petty.

"This family, K.O., are descended from the king. Maybe that's not important to you, but it is to them. To us."

K.O. had never seen him so intense. She started to reply, but he cut her off.

"If you were a descendant from European royalty, a *haole* queen, I bet you'd think that was pretty great, wouldn't you?" He was really angry.

There was, in fact, some rumor in K.O.'s family that they were descended from the Irish royal family, but she didn't put much store in that, and actually thought it not prudent to bring up at this moment.

Maybe that was the problem. Even if she were related to royalty, it meant nothing to her, because she and her whole family were so removed from their Irish roots.

Here in Hawai'i, however, people stayed close, traced the generations and lineages. Most of that was due to pride and honor, but unfortunately, some of it was for legal reasons. Hawaiian Homelands went to Hawaiians. Other privileges did as well.

She scrambled to recall what she'd read. One had to be fifty percent Hawaiian, and traceable at that, to receive the perks.

Alani continued. "I arranged a fundraising concert with Kalapana to play, and I am supposed to be there. I have the musicians coming, sound and lights, caterers—everything—because *I* set it up. They are counting on me. I came here at your request. What do you want?"

K.O. did not know this person who sat across from her. She wondered how she had ever thought she did. It made her inexorably sad.

"I, uh," she began. What could she say? *I'm trying to clear your name, but between you and me, you look really guilty. Basically, I guess I'm trying to solve the case, even if it's at your expense?* Great, K.O. Way to go.

She tried again. "I had some questions, but I guess you answered them." *It sounds as if you'd do anything to further your cause, and that this whole mess is tied to the Homelands.*

"I'm glad I could be of help." Alani's stone-face broke into a smile again, and K.O.'s heart lifted a little.

The smile was for Cherry.

"Here you go." She put down two huge, brimming plates.

"Can you put mine in a package for me?" Alani asked. "I'm sorry, Cherry, but I have someplace to be."

"Too bad it's not here," Cherry joked with a wink.

Yeah, agreed K.O silently. *Too bad it's not anywhere with me.*

Cherry took Alani's plate back to the kitchen. K.O. met his gaze. Her heart broke. He looked nearly as miserable as she felt.

"K.O. I have to go. I'm sorry."

For what? She wanted to scream at him. *For leaving the meal? For leaving me? For killing one, maybe two men?*

For what? All she said was, "Me, too." She felt tears well up but refused to let them fall.

Alani stood. "I'll get this. You stay and finish."

K.O. didn't know what he meant until he moved to the cash register with the check. He bestowed another gleaming smile on Cherry who materialized with his Styrofoam box. She said something and he laughed, accepting his change with a smile as Cherry unnecessarily brushed his hand.

"Oh, I think we're finished," K.O. mumbled to herself and rose from the table, leaving more than her meal to cool and turn to rubbish.

CHAPTER TWENTY-FIVE

K.O. was so upset, she nearly missed it.

She was driving back to Waikiki to visit Abby and Richard, as promised. She had shopped for them blindly in the Time's market underneath King's coffee shop, throwing items in her basket, unaware of her purchases.

Alani and her last conversation played in her head, interspersed randomly with flashes of reports, crime scenes, other conversations. Then, just as she passed Kanekapolei Street on the Ala Wai Canal, it hit her.

The key. The thing that held the whole mess together.

She screeched across three lanes of traffic to stop along the canal and park. She got out a notebook and turned to a fresh page.

She wrote Hawaiian Homelands in big letters in the middle, and circled it. Then she wrote out from the center, like spokes of a wheel, all the factors that had come up in recent days—Alani; HCS; *Ka Leo;* timeshares; Larry Ellis; Blala Richards—until she had filled the page with lines. She added in very small print, what she knew about each spoke. Unfortunately, that part was extremely sketchy. She was still missing a piece that made the wheel make sense. The only connection between the timeshares and Homelands was Kepa, but she was sure she was right.

The Hawaiian Homelands issue was at stake, and at center. Unfortunately, when it came to the Homelands, Alani was involved up to his neck.

A sharp knock at her window startled her. She looked up, ready with a retort, and saw a blue uniform. She rolled down her window, realizing with some chagrin that her engine was still running.

"Hi, Horace."

"Oh, K.O., it's you. I was wondering what *lolo* parked all *kapakahi* in a red zone, half in the intersection, with the engine running. Figures." He was smiling.

"Sorry, eh? I was working on a case." She showed her drawing by way of explanation, which she knew meant nothing to the patrolman. She felt pretty stupid, now that she noticed her car was parked partly in a red zone and not quite clear of the intersection at Walina street.

"Lucky you nevah get rear-ended," he scolded.

"For reals. Sorry. I'm going, now."

He shook his head and waved a hand in dismissal, turning back to his beat car.

She put her car in gear but discovered she was angled into the curb. To add to her chagrin, she had to reverse a couple feet, while Horace stood in the traffic lane, directing cars into the next lane.

Finally free, she rolled down her window and held out a hand in "shaka," fist with thumb and pinky extended, and shook it to say thank you. Horace was laughing as he returned to his vehicle.

K.O. was sweating with embarrassment. She vowed to pay more attention to her driving and carefully navigated to Abby's and Richard's hotel.

She parked in the miniscule underground garage and hefted her two heavy grocery bags to the elevator.

"What the hell did I buy? Bricks?"

The car dinged and stopped. She tottered out with her

increasingly heavy burden to the room farthest from the elevator and knocked.

From inside she heard shuffling footsteps that took forever to come. She was about to put down her bags when Abby opened the door.

Surprised it wasn't Richard, K.O. saw Abby's pale face in the gap. She put down her shopping and gently pushed on the door. "What's wrong, Abby?"

The door swung open without resistance. Abby swayed unsteadily, and K.O. grabbed her arm.

"What, Abby? What is it?"

"It's Richard." Abby looked towards the sitting room, and K.O. shot forward.

Richard sat in the recliner—pale, sweating, eyes closed.

"Richard. It's K.O. What's wrong?" She knelt at his side and took his pulse. Erratic.

"Hi, hon. Don't feel so good. My arm hurts."

"Okay, Richard. Sit tight. We're gonna fix you right up." She dived for the phone and called 911, requesting an ambulance for a possible heart attack. Even if that wasn't what it turned out to be, she reasoned, the ambulance would respond faster to a cardio-pulmonary episode.

Abby still leaned against the wall in the entry way, the door open, like a moment frozen in time. The odd artificial light spilled in from the hall, casting her as a plastic statue.

"Abby, come sit down with Richard. Here, hold his hand." K.O. guided the stricken woman to a chair she had pulled next to Richard's.

Abby mechanically did as she was told. K.O. covered them both with blankets, elevated feet, and monitored their pulses in the eternity it took for the ambulance crew to arrive. By then, she had gone through the luggage and bathroom cupboards, dumping all the medications she could find into a sack.

The room filled with personnel, bustle, voices. K.O. took

Abby's purse and Richard's wallet and numbly followed the crew, swirling in their wake, downstairs to the waiting vehicle.

She knew she had answered all their questions correctly because their faces indicated as much, but she could not have repeated what she'd said if someone had held a gun to her head.

She followed the ambulance to Queen's Hospital downtown, a stone's throw from HPD. To curb her mounting fear, she focused on what it would be like in a couple hours from now: Abby and Richard admitted to the hospital, finished with emergency procedures, quietly resting, watching TV game shows and eating Jello. Sharing a room and . . . what? K.O. didn't know, but she had run out of options and time. She pulled into the ER lot and plunged into the chaos at Queen's emergency. She didn't realize it, but she had not stopped praying since she had left the groceries in the hotel hall.

CHAPTER TWENTY-SIX

Again, it was the newspaper that informed the islands, including Donna, of the latest.

"Damn it! K.O.'s gonna be pissed." Donna dialed K.O.'s office. *Voice mail.*

Next she left a message on her pager.

She read the headline again. PRESIDENT OF HCS, NAHUA, ARRESTED ON MONEY LAUNDERING CHARGES.

The story went on to say that the timeshare condos had been under investigation for months, and Kepa Nahua, along with several others, had been arrested. She was unfamiliar with the other arrestees. The Hawaiian Cultural Society was also under investigation for money laundering.

That puzzled Donna. Even she knew the radical group *Ka Leo* was much more likely to launder funds, and through such convoluted means as to make it nearly impossible to trace. Why would so many legitimate Hawaiians—or so she thought, she amended—associate with something so underhanded? It would only jeopardize their cause.

Unless, she reasoned, there were two groups inside the HCS. One, who truly wanted what they felt was best for native

Hawaiians, and used education and sharing of Aloha as their vehicle, and a second group, who wanted . . . what?—Money? Power?—and was willing to sacrifice its own people to that end. It all circled fuzzily in her brain.

"Call me, K.O.!"

Donna wanted to run her ideas past her friend. She glanced at the clock and thought K.O. should be getting to work pretty soon.

She drew a Venn diagram on the back of a draft of a report. Two interlocking circles. In one she wrote HCS and in the other she wrote *Ka Leo*. She shaded the central ellipse gray and wrote "Homelands." How could she check on connections? What tied them together besides the obvious: Kepa Nahua?

"Jeez, K.O. I'm glad it's not an emergency!" she called out loud to no one. She stood and stretched, mentally and physically shaking herself out of it.

She took a bathroom break. When she returned, Tiny stood in front of her desk, report in hand.

"Just dropping this off, Boss." He tossed a report onto the pile.

"Thanks, Tiny. Howzit going?"

"Fine. Gotta go." Tiny left her office without further comment.

"Okee doke." Donna watched him go. Usually he was laughing, always joking. *Maybe just tired,* she thought.

She sat back at her desk and took the report Tiny had just left. It sat on top of the Venn diagram she had drawn. She had left it face up, hadn't she? Now it was down. Maybe that was what had got him all up tight. He was Hawaiian. Maybe he was as upset by all of this as she was.

He really was a sweetheart, she mused. *I'll have to ask him about it. I guess I have been kind of wrapped up and insensitive about it. To me, it's a case, a puzzle, but to him, maybe it's a little closer.*

The phone rang and she pounced. "Medical examiner . . . K.O.!"

CHAPTER TWENTY-SEVEN

K.O. sat in the waiting room at Queen's emergency. Abby and Richard had been swept away, and she'd been booted from their room ages ago. She'd retrieved her briefcase from her car and made the appropriate phone calls about being late to work.

She had asked for news for the zillionth time, and now the hospital staff were getting testy with her.

"We'll tell you when we know something. For now they're stable." The nurse glared at her, and K.O. couldn't blame her. New cases had come and gone with varying degrees of severity. Bleeding. Fevers. Ambiguous pains. Lonely people wanting attention.

She had been told that Abby and Richard would be admitted for observation, but she couldn't get any more information than that. She decided to take a walk and stretch her legs.

"I'm just going for a quick walk, okay?" she told the least cranky of the nurses she'd been pestering. "Here's my pager number. Call me if you can tell me anything. Please?"

"Yes. We will." The nurse looked relieved that K.O. was leaving, if only temporarily.

K.O. went out the big doors into the humid afternoon. It was later than she'd thought, the sky graying with impending sunset. The odd combination of the smells of plumeria, so sweet and heavy, with the carbon monoxide of too many cars downtown made her feel a little nauseated. Maybe it was just the stress, she reasoned. *Did I eat?*

She hadn't. She couldn't remember even eating breakfast, but she must have, right? God, this morning seemed so long ago. She was so tired. She felt the weight of the day, and of the cases pressing on her. She was ready to weep.

Instead, she went to a nearby noodle shop on Alapai street and had a bowl of noodles with tofu and vegetables. A pot of green tea steamed at her elbow. She watched several old men arguing in Mandarin about their mah-jongg game. Although she couldn't understand the words, she did understand that the friendly squabbling was probably a weekly, if not a daily, ritual in this little shop: an island of quiet in the storm of traffic and chaos just outside the door. The jangle of the front door and invasion of sound coincided with her pager going off, and at first, she didn't recognize the sound.

A spurt of adrenaline coursed into her stomach, churning her meal. She checked the number and immediately calmed when she saw it was Donna Costello from the M.E.'s office.

She sat for another few minutes, finishing her tea, listening once again to the clicking of tiles and wrangling over scores or wins. Whatever. She didn't know the game, but found the experience soothing.

Sufficiently restored, she paid her bill, said thank you to the lady behind the register, and to her own surprise and theirs, to the old mah-jongg men. They bobbed their heads and smiled snaggle-toothed grins at her, clearly indicating that this foreign woman was too strange, and possibly too dangerous, to ignore.

This made K.O. smile even wider as she made her way back to Queen's Hospital and to the pay phone to return Donna's call.

"Hey, Donna. It's K.O. What's up?"

"Did you read the paper? I can't believe it!"

"No, I've been kinda busy. What?" K.O. wondered what in the world had transpired while she'd been consumed with Abby and Richard.

"Kepa Nahua's been arrested!"

"Right on! Alani's one step closer to being off the hook." K.O.'s spirits lifted slightly as the depression of the day swam around her.

"Not so fast. He wasn't arrested for murder. He was arrested for money laundering. The whole of HCS is under investigation, too."

"Wait! HCS, not *Ka Leo?*"

"Yup. I knew you'd be mad. I haven't called Roly yet. I wonder what Homicide thinks."

"I can just bet they are all fired up. When I talked to him the other day, he wasn't sure what was going on with Nahua and the timeshare scheme. He thought they were close to making an arrest, but I know he wanted in on it for those murders."

"Give him a call and let me know."

"I will. I bet they'd rather get Nahua on all the money counts because they've been building this case for so long. So that means they're gonna be looking harder at Alani for the murders. They like Alani for this local stuff. You know, Alani told me that Richards and Nahua were arguing over the Aloha Week publicity budget. That Nahua really wanted to do something big and was trying to generate big bucks for it. Richards wasn't supporting him, and Alani thought that was weird. That must have been something to do with the money laundering. You know, trouble in paradise."

"What a mess."

"You said it. Like I don't have enough right now."

"What else?"

"I'm at Queen's ER right now. I told you about those friends of my mom's who are visiting the islands, yeah? Well, they bought a timeshare from Kepa Nahua. I'm trying to sort it all out, but the contract looks good. Anyway"—K.O. tried to pull her jumbled thoughts together—"the stress gave Richard a heart attack or something. Abby went into shock. I'm at my wits end." K.O. heard the tremble in her voice and took a deep breath.

"I'll come down."

"You can't. You have too much to do."

"Shut up. I can. I have eight thousand comp hours I can take, and I'm taking one to be with my friend."

"No. That's okay. I'm just waiting here until they tell me their conditions. Then I have to go to work."

They talked for a while longer, and Donna hung up. K.O. felt a little better. Oddly, when she had told Donna not to come down, she really hadn't wanted her to, but now that Donna wasn't coming, she wished she were. *I'm just bizarre,* K.O. thought. It really would feel good to run the case—well, cases, she corrected herself—by her friend. A good distraction and the benefit of Donna's professional insight.

A figure in hospital scrubs approached her. "Ms. Ogden? I have news for you."

K.O. glanced up from her perch on the sticky vinyl bench. She studied the nurse's face for clues before nodding. She didn't look ready to tell the worst. Wouldn't a doctor have come out and done that part, anyway?

K.O. stood. "Yes?"

"I'll take you up to them."

Relief flooded her. If they were really bad off, she wouldn't be able to visit, right?

As they walked, the nurse filled her in. Richard—mild heart attack, stable, resting. Abby—treated for shock, should be fine. But they seemed to want to stay together, so the doc had approved an overnight for her. Richard needed meds, care, maybe surgery. That part of the conversation floated somewhere above K.O.'s head. They were okay.

"Can Richard's surgery wait until he gets home? Can he travel?"

"The doctor will fill you in on all that. Here we are."

She pushed open the overlarge door and K.O. saw two bundles in two twin beds. Richard looked a little gray, but gave her a hearty smile. Abby's bright eyes peered out of the blankets, her snowy hair in tufts, making her look even more like a nesting bird. She was smiling.

"Hi, kids. You gave me quite a scare, you two." K.O. bent and kissed each one.

"Hi, Katrina. Richard's going to be fine, they said."

"Yes, he is," K.O. said firmly. She sat in the straight-backed chair between the beds and held their hands across the gap.

"As soon as you're okay to travel, you should see your own doc in Seattle, right?" She looked at Richard.

"Yes, Katrina. That's what they tell me."

"How are you doing?"

"I feel better, but tired."

"Well, I have some good news for you." Both of her elderly charges perked up.

"Yes?"

"They've arrested that bad guy about the timeshares, so it looks like you'll eventually get at least some of your money back."

She watched them process this and slowly smile. They exchanged a glance and once again, K.O. was reminded how strong was their bond.

"See, Richard? I knew that would work out!" Abby squeezed K.O.'s hand, and K.O. passed the squeeze gently on to Richard. He smiled.

K.O. vowed she would pay them herself if she had to. She had no information, or even real hope, that the timeshare company could be forced to make restitution to clients. She wondered how much the couple had paid and how much of an equity line she could draw off her condo.

Her stomach lurched at the thought of going into debt, but when she looked at them gazing at each other with such love and adoration, herself in the middle, connected by a frail hand on each side, a sense of calm poured over her.

"I'm going to talk to your doctor and find out how to get you two on a plane back home."

"We're cheaper if we're cargo," said Richard, with a hint of his former rascally self.

"Oh, Richard. You are such a card." Abby giggled, and K.O. laughed. *All these years, and Abby still thinks he's funny. Will miracles never cease?*

She kissed them both once again and told Richard to stay out of Abby's bed. Abby blushed and Richard waggled his silver eyebrows.

K.O. found the nurse's station and hunted down the doctor. After a lengthy chat he determined that Richard could go home in a few days if all progressed as expected. He had already contacted Richard's doctor in Washington.

As she listened, K.O. felt a great weight lift. Richard and Abby back at home and no longer her responsibility. The condo thing resolved . . . sort of.

Gee, only a couple of homicides left to deal with, and I'm home free!

She didn't want to think about what that resolution might mean for her relationship with Alani. She had a pain in her chest that had nothing to do with her health.

She got her car and headed back to HPD. She passed the newsboys in the traffic lanes as they hawked papers at red lights. She waved a child over and handed him a dollar just as the light changed to green. She didn't wait for her change as she pulled away after glancing at the headline.

Great. Just great. She knew she could figure out this puzzle. And she also knew what the cost would be. Even if she "won," she would lose.

CHAPTER TWENTY-EIGHT

Back in her office, and very late for her shift, K.O. chugged half a Diet Pepsi. Then, her priorities taken care of, she efficiently addressed the new stack of pink message slips, checked and logged evidence, wrote and reviewed reports. Several hours passed this way, and her mind never stopped turning over the Homelands case.

She wanted to confront Alani, but what good would it do? He was already guarded, their former closeness evaporated like morning mist. Once again, she felt cheated, thinking maybe she'd been wrong about that, too.

She knew what he'd told her. He'd joined the Hawaiian Cultural Society to promote Hawaiian culture and customs. He'd become involved in the Homelands issue gradually, drawn in by a series of circumstances, and now was unable to extract himself from the more radical side of things. Yes, she knew what he'd said. She would have believed anything even a week ago, but now? She was back to her prickly, suspicious self, unable to shake the feeling that she'd been a sucker. That hurt most of all.

The stubborn side of her, however, was unable to let the case go. Too many threads tied her to it, and she had to sit patiently in the middle, unwinding each strand to its end.

God, I drive myself crazy, she thought. She laughed ruefully and decided she'd earned a break.

Her idea of a break was to call Roly in Homicide. *I'm just a party girl,* she sighed, dialing.

"Homicide."

"Hey, Lt. Lee, howzit? K.O. in Evidence. Roly around?"

"Yeah. Try wait." She was put on hold briefly.

"Yo, K.O., what's up?" Roly's voice was brisk and youthful. She pictured the small detective relaxed but immaculate, no matter what the case or time of day.

"I called with my condolences about the Nahua arrest."

"Very funny, K.O."

K.O. remembered their last conversation had ended somewhat shakily, and not only did she not want to upset this kind man, she wanted him on her side. "No, Roly. I'm serious. I know how hard you've been working on those homicides, and you know—with the Alani thing and all—I just wanted to say I'm sorry. I know how hard it can be. You set up a whole case and some other agency swoops in and scoops you and all your work."

"Yeah. Thanks, K.O." He sounded a bit mollified.

"So, do you know what happened?"

"Not really. They're not talking. We didn't really have enough evidence to arrest yet. No physical, but a lot of circumstantial. We were putting together a case when—pack!" K.O. heard a slapping sound and assumed he'd smacked one hand to another like a hand to the head. "I know you wanted Nahua to swing for the murders to clear your friend, and I think he's good for them, too. I think he's mixed up in the whole mess, but we might have a hard time connecting him to it."

"I know what you mean. I've been losing sleep over this whole thing. Nahua's in the middle, right? With *Ka Leo*, HCS, and the Homelands all in there, too?"

"Yeah. The Feds think Nahua was washing money for *Ka Leo,*

through HCS. The sovereignty task force thinks they're buying weapons, vehicles, amassing property through legitimate citizens for the big 'take over.' When they secede from the U.S. or some shit. You know these fundraisers he does all the time, including that one for the homestead family? Well, he has a legit organization to make money, HCS, but the money's funneled into *Ka Leo*. He does the same thing with the timeshares. It's such a scam. He gets people's money and it goes into *Ka Leo,* which also means it goes to him."

"And you guys got involved because of the Ellis murder?"

"Yeah, but we think he's responsible for other 'mysterious' deaths. Contract hits, maybe. But he's good. We've been watching him for a while, but have a hard time catching the guy. Nahua murdering Richards doesn't make sense to me unless they had a falling out, which is possible."

"Are you guys gonna keep investigating Nahua in conjunction with those homicides?"

"Yes, mom. We haven't solved them, and they are the two biggest cases we've had since Imelda Marcos's shoe theft."

"Someone stole Imelda's shoes?"

"Cheez, K.O. No. Gimme a break."

K.O. laughed. "You crack me, up. Seriously, if it's not Nahua, and it's not Alani, then we're all missing something."

Roly sighed heavily. "K.O. I can't tell you something I don't know. Even if I know, I'm not *supposed* to tell you."

"Yes, but you love me and you just can't help yourself." K.O. thought she heard him mumble something about needing a drink. "Roly, these timeshares and Nahua have messed with a number of my friends, and I'm not going to let this go. I can see I'm missing something, and it's right in front of me. It's driving me nuts."

"When you figure it out, give me a call. In the mean time, I got other cases and Lee's breathing down my neck."

"'Kay. Thanks Roly, for your time and support. I'm going over the cases and reports again. Donna's been great and this is bugging her, too. Sometimes a case just gets to you, you know?"

"Yeah, I know."

K.O. hung up, thoughtful. It was possible that Nahua wasn't responsible—directly anyway—for the two homicides. She was sure they'd been committed by the same person, probably male, given Blala Richards's size and mana. He had been powerful physically, but she had experienced something else in his presence.

Richards had been stabbed. A close-up killing. No small person, male or female, could have done that. No drugs in Richards's body, no sedatives, no alcohol, nothing to slow him, stun him, control him. Just sheer power, anger, fear—something—had taken him out.

Nahua could have contracted a hit. Who in the islands was connected and big enough? More than one person? Possible, but the crime scene didn't indicate more than one assailant. She couldn't rule it out completely, though.

I have to go on my gut that says Alani didn't do it either, or else what have I got?

Realistically, he could have, if enraged enough. He was over six feet tall, with strong hands and shoulders from working wood and paddling a canoe. But he was also slender. Richards had outweighed him by a hundred pounds.

Alani could have surprised him, snuck up and done him. But that would mean they had known each other. It had happened in Richards's apartment. But wait, they had known each other. Alani had admitted that. So, it was possible.

K.O. put her head in her hands and rested her aching neck. Under her desk, between her feet, the day's paper had slipped to the floor. She saw again the headline and story of the arrest, but something else caught her eye. Another follow-up story on the Kaneali'ihiwi family's plight. She picked up the paper and read that article.

It featured the grandfather, a handsome Hawaiian man in his sixties, as he told of the history of the land and how it had been handed down, generation to generation. His photo showed him in motion, gesturing passionately as he talked, seated in a living room filled with family photos and heirlooms: heavy stone *poi-pounders*, shark's tooth clubs, tools, carvings, pictures.

His face was somehow familiar, but K.O. decided it was just so much news coverage. The family had been interviewed by every news station in the islands, but K.O.'s favorite interview had been with Joe Moore. Joe was a great guy and made people feel like he cared. He also had a wicked sense of humor.

K.O. cut out both stories and added them to her bulging case file. She paged through the newspaper again to see if she'd missed anything.

Not that she could tell.

Her eyes burned and she felt drained. Still, she knew she'd better turn her attention to what she was getting paid for. She worked for several more hours, late into the night, on evidence and logs, forcing herself to focus on the job at hand. Like a song that wouldn't leave her head, the image of the senior Kaneali'ihiwi, his hands fluttering and dancing in conversation, his face questioning and pleading, remained with her.

CHAPTER TWENTY-NINE

K.O.'s sleep was plagued with the Homelands case, but when she awoke a little later than usual, she felt pretty good, inspired even.

She fed Teresa-kitty her breakfast, apologized for the felonious feline neglect, and sailed out the door with her silver HPD travel mug brimming with extra-strength coffee.

She drove up the coast on the two-lane highway admiring the teal-colored ocean just feet to her right, and the emerald mountains soaring to the clouds on her left. She made it to the Kaneali'ihiwi homesite and wondered if she should have called first.

Way too late now. It wasn't too early for a house call, she reasoned, but she was still trepidatious as she approached the front door.

The wrap-around front lanai looked just as it had in the news coverage, but the foliage surrounding the house was much lusher and more beautiful than it had appeared.

She passed the *koa* rockers and rack with shoes and slippers. The windows seemed dark in the bright morning, and the curtains didn't move although the screens were open. Shavings from wood and sawdust reminded K.O. of visits to Alani's workshop and reinforced her loss. A partially carved section of palm trunk sat in front of a stool, as if the artist had left just moments ago.

She didn't have time to observe further because the door creaked open and she recognized the shadowy features of Mr. Kaneali'ihiwi.

"What you want?"

K.O. was taken aback by his tone, but not necessarily surprised. He must have suffered countless intrusions the past weeks.

"Hello, sir. I'm K.O., Katrina Ogden, and I . . . ." she trailed off because she hadn't thought this far ahead. She had no official standing investigating the case, and she wasn't even sure if she wanted to tell him she was with the police department. Merely standing on his porch seemed invasive enough and she blushed as she remembered her *haole* status.

He had said nothing, moving not an inch. She could not see beyond him into the interior of the dark house. It bothered her a little, not knowing if he was armed, or if someone else waited just inside.

She cleared her throat and tried again, deciding to go with the truth and ask for his help. "I don't have any official reason to be here, sir. But your case, your problem, has involved some friends of mine, particularly one who has been helping you. He's now in big trouble, and I want to help him. I just don't know how, and I'm hoping you will help me."

She had said all this in one rush of breath, and stood waiting, peering into the dark. Mr. Kaneali'ihiwi's face had all but disappeared in shadow. After several moments of eerie silence, he asked gruffly, "Who?"

"Alani Okita."

"'Kay, den." The door opened wider, and he stepped out onto the porch. He was a much larger man than she had thought, over six feet tall, and just as powerful in the upper body as Alani. His mana was strong, and she involuntarily stepped away, maintaining a distance.

He wore an old T-shirt, stained with what looked like paint or wood varnish. Ratty shorts and rubber slippers from the shoe rack completed his attire. He was a striking man, however. His cropped silver hair, thick and wavy, was combed away from his face. If he had been wearing royal robes, he would not have looked more regal.

He studied her and made some kind of private assessment, because he nodded, more to himself than her, and said, "Sit," pointing to one of the rockers.

He sat on the stool fronting the palm trunk and ran his hands expertly over the rough outlines.

"What are you making?" K.O. had not intended to ask, but seeing him with the wood brought it out.

He cocked his head, his hands stilled. "Ku."

K.O. knew that Ku was one of the pantheon of Hawaiian gods and realized he was making an image into a tiki; however, she did not know which god Ku was.

"Ku?" she asked.

His eyes locked with hers, and he did not move. She felt immobilized but not altogether uncomfortable. She exhaled slowly, feeling calmer, and waited, allowing the examination.

"God of war. Human sacrifice."

"Oh." K.O. swallowed. *Not good.*

He smiled at her. A warm smile with white teeth. "And other things: canoe-building, the forest. Create, destroy. It's all balance."

He pulled a chisel out of one of his pockets, picked up a block of wood for a hammer, and began to carve. "So, what did you want?"

K.O. could move again. She felt better. Maybe not entirely safe, but okay for now.

"As I said, my friend Alani has been trying to help you folks and so have other people. Now Alani's in trouble. They think he murdered Blala Richards, and I am trying to find evidence to clear him."

"Evidence, eh?" He paused in his work. "Sounds official."

"It's not. I mean, I *am,* but he's just my friend."

He began to carve again. "I see. I t'ink he's more den your friend, but you right. He's in big trouble."

"Everywhere I look, it seems to come back to you."

"What chu mean, me?"

"Well, not you personally, I don't think. I mean the Homelands issue."

"What about it?"

"I think I need to begin at the beginning." K.O. took a big breath.

"Usually a good place."

K.O. heard his amusement and let out the air. She tried to keep things in sequence, tried to keep her emotions out as she relayed everything she could that wouldn't compromise the open cases.

"I guess the HCS is trying to help you, too, but Kepa Nahua has been arrested for the timeshare thing, and my auntie and uncle"—K.O. used the universal honorifics for unofficial family—"bought one, and they no can afford 'em." Her pidgin intensified as she finished her story. "I just don't know where else to go, 'cause everything led to you."

K.O. felt tears of frustration and anger well up, and she blinked furiously. *Way to go Ogden, let your emotions totally cloud the issue.* "So, I came to you," she finished lamely.

Throughout her monologue, he had worked steadily, and the figure of the god Ku had taken shape and form. He had taken a chunk of wood and, without her seeing how he did it, had removed the material that wasn't Ku.

He set down his tools. "I got news for you. Dat Nahua is no good. He is not helping us. He is bad. We nevah ask fo' his help, and he nevah give it 'til two weeks ago. Dat's when all da problem start. We been fighting for our land for more den a year, but only now everybody t'inks it started."

His black eyes were intense, and K.O. believed him.

Ellis's murder had caused something to change. Why? "What do you know about the golf-course thing?"

"Not'ting. Got not'ting to do wit' us. Dey can't sell our land to the golf people. It's in the Constitution."

"So what, then? What is it? Larry Ellis was murdered for what?"

"Das da *haole* guy in da cave, yeah?"

"Yeah."

"Some sick guy want us to t'ink it's a *haole* t'ing. It's not. Somebody knew exactly what he's doing to cause a war."

"Are you saying it's a Hawaiian who put that body in the cave? Why? Why such sacrilege?"

"Hey, even Hawaiians go crazy sometime." His smile was grim.

"Do you know something? Are you sure?"

"I cannot say."

"Can't or won't?"

He shrugged and picked up his tools.

"But I'm trying to help!" K.O. stood in frustration. "Please, help me to help Alani and you."

"I goin' be all right. Whatever happens, we goin' be all right."

"You could lose your land! Don't you even care?"

He stood and his eyes filled with fire. "You don't know anything, girl. Remember dat! I know dis land will nevah be a golf course, no matter who is living here. Das all dat matters. Alani goin' need you, so you help him. I don't need your help. I take care of my own. My family for hundreds of years didn't need your help."

He opened the screen door, his face softening a little. "You mean well, seestah, I know dat. You a good person, and I will remember dat. I can't help you more den I have. T'ings gonna be da way dey's gonna be," he muttered cryptically and stepped inside.

The screen slammed, and the inner door clicked shut.

K.O. was left on the porch with the fierce Ku, wondering what help she had been given. She felt stupid. She had even more pieces to the puzzle, she was sure of it, but not *the* piece. In her gut, she knew it was all laid out for her; Mr. Kaneali'ihiwi had told her what she needed, perhaps at his own peril, but it was in code. A secret.

"Too many goddamn secrets," she threw over her shoulder to Ku as she stomped to her car. "All locks and no keys."

She thought she heard laughter from inside the house follow her across the yard, but when she turned to look, only a curtain blew in the window.

CHAPTER THIRTY

K.O. drove to work the long way. From the tiny town of Haleiwa, she took the H-2 south, pondering her findings.

Everyone thought this whole mess had started with Larry Ellis's murder. Mr. Kaneali'ihiwi said it hadn't. He said it had started over a year before.

What if that was the case? She would have to find out who was involved a year ago. *Great.*

Her brain reeled at the thought of unraveling the two key organizations from a year ago. She was a thorough police officer, which was why she had been encouraged to try for the Sergeant's Exam. So she would do the research if she had to, but her gut— also a keen detecting tool—told her she'd already been given the necessary information. She just had to flail around blindly until it all fell into place.

She laughed imagining the headline: OFFICER OGDEN SOLVES CASE BY DILIGENT FLAILING.

The H-2 freeway traffic merged, then slowed onto the H-1, giving her plenty of time to observe the blue Pacific, looking southwest to Makaha where Ellis's body had been discovered.

She mentally went over her lists of people, evidence, and reports as she inched towards Honolulu.

Another click in her brain said she needed to recheck the evidence. After all, that's what she did best right now. Evidence. She had been given a pile of it by Kimo and Donna, which she had carefully filed away. Now she felt compelled to look at it all again.

Frustrated, she cranked up the rock station on the radio and sang with Bad Company, until she finally pulled into the station, grabbed her stuff, and headed to the office. She automatically greeted her friends and co-workers, but was determined not to become distracted.

She entered the large Evidence area and went directly to the shelves containing the relevant cases. She brought out large bags, labeled with the case numbers, and set them in a well-lit examination area.

Something immediately caught her eye. She would look at everything, of course, but what she'd noticed was the murder weapon from Blala Richards's case.

The wood chisel. A unique design, an antique, which Alani had said was a gift from an old friend—another carver, and his mentor.

It exactly matched the chisel Mr. Kaneali'ihiwi had used to create Ku.

K.O. didn't know much about wood carving or its tools, but she did know evidence. She knew the tools were as identical as they could be and not be the same tool. She would have to ask a number of questions.

For Kimo in SIS: Was it indisputable that *this* tool was the murder weapon? In other words, could there be reasonable doubt?

For Alani: Was he positive that this tool was his tool? And had Mr. Kaneali'ihiwi given it to him? Was he the mentor and gift-giver?

And for anyone who would tell her the truth: Could there be a third chisel to the set?

The truth was becoming more muddled. Someone was being protected here, and she didn't know who or why. Someone connected to the Hawaiian Sovereignty issue. For or against it, she didn't know either, but if she had understood Mr. Kealiʻiihiwi correctly, he thought the murderer was Hawaiian, and working for his own end, but using the HCS and *Ka Leo* to do it.

She knew Alani's chisel was missing. She knew he had been found covered in blood that had only proven to be his own. She knew the murder weapon matched his, was purported to be his, but had only Richards's blood on it. She knew Homicide and Evidence said this chisel was Alani's and Alani couldn't say it wasn't. The crime revealed careful planning and inside knowledge of a number of things: Hawaiiana; wood carving; HCS; and *Ka Leo;* crime scene information to make two connected murders seem unrelated.

The only thing she was sure of was that Alani appeared guilty, but that he was not guilty. He couldn't be. Because that would mean she had loved a murderer, and that was something she didn't think she could live with.

She replaced all the items in their proper bags, labels and all, and returned them to the shelves in the Evidence room.

Just as she returned to her desk, Selena buzzed her with a phone call.

"Evidence, Ogden."

"K.O. It's Alani."

She would have known his voice anywhere. "Hi, Alani. I was just thinking about you. Wondering how you were doing."

"I called to ask you something. I thought I was doing pretty good, you know, keeping my spirits up, but I heard something I needed to check out."

K.O.'s heartbeat sped up, and she felt decidedly queasy. "Yeah, what's up? I've been working on your case, and I have a question for you, too."

"That's what I wanted to ask you. Along with working on my

case, I heard that I wouldn't even *be* a case if it weren't for you."

K.O. heard the controlled anger in his voice. She had seen the face that went with that voice far too often lately. "I, uh, meant to talk to you about that."

"Really? And what stopped you?"

"Alani, I'm sorry. I thought I was doing the right thing."

"Having me arrested for murder seemed like the right thing? Jeez, K.O. I thought we were friends."

"It wasn't supposed to go like that." All the emotion of that night came reeling back in a tidal wave. The rain. Her anticipation of romance. Okay—of love. Everything she had said she wanted in a relationship coming to pass, and then washing out instantly. She was hurt, angry, afraid all over again.

"Yeah? Well, we were not friends!" she shouted into the phone. "I thought we were more than friends. I was in love with you!"

Supreme silence. K.O.'s adrenaline had dumped, and she was sweaty. The phone clasped tightly in one hand, the other covering her eyes, tears streaming, nose running, she waited, ashamed and embarrassed.

"K.O. I'm sorry." She heard a deep breath. "I didn't know."

"How could you not know?" Her voice, small and raw, had lost its ferocity. She was empty now, truly empty. "How could you not know?" She groped for a tissue and blotted her face.

She wished she were on top of a mountain so she could wail, scream, shout. She was grieving. Again. She crumpled up the tissue and heaved it onto the floor. She looked out her window into the main office. Selena had herded the other clerks into the far corner by the file cabinet and was distributing papers, bless her. K.O. was grateful that Selena had tried to shield her emotional display of personal grief from the office and its microcosm of gossip. She took a shaky breath.

"I know it doesn't seem like it now, and you can believe me or not, but despite all my personal feelings, and they are considerable, I don't think you killed anyone."

Alani just breathed for a moment, and K.O. knew he was grasping the receiver as tightly as she was, trying to collect himself. "Thank you. I didn't. Please, just tell me, what happened?"

K.O.'s skin was icy. *I might never be warm again,* she thought. She detached herself as best she could. "I overheard your phone conversation that night. I found out too many things that didn't add up. I also made a poor decision to tell Homicide, rather than confront you about it. I never intended for you to get arrested, but that's what happened."

"What conversation?"

"You were having words with Kepa Nahua, and it was related to the Ellis murder. You sounded like an accessory, either before or after, and I couldn't let it lie."

"K.O. I never . . ."

She forged ahead. "Also, I came to your house late that night, in a raging storm, for a date. A dinner, prepared by you. Flowers, wine, a card for Chrissake! And I find out that you had no romantic intentions. I felt completely used. I felt . . . undesirable." She pressed back the ache in her soul and continued. "Undesired." She had just peeled off her skin and laid it on the floor. She had never felt more vulnerable, more weaponless in her life.

"Oh, K.O. No. I meant . . . I mean, I was interested in you. That's why I invited you. I wanted to be with you."

Another vast silence. K.O. picked up her skin, her armor, even more scarred than ever, and put it back on. "It doesn't matter now." *It so doesn't matter now. It's too late.*

"I am going to help you. I have been working on your case. Just tell me what that call was about."

"I do fundraising for the cause. I donate my bowls for auction, I donate my time. I was also starting to work with the Lt. Governor's office on behalf of the Hawaiian Nation. I'm respected in the business and art communities as well as the Hawaiian community. Kepa wanted that for the people, the movement. He knows how he's viewed and wanted me to help."

"Why you? How do you know him?"

"We went to school together. Way back. Small-kid time. We were friends, once. I also know how he's viewed, and if I could do something to make things more positive, help improve relations between us and the government, I wanted to do it."

Alani sighed. "I was just starting to meet with the movers and shakers, including Larry Ellis, when he was murdered. I got nervous, that's all."

A few pieces clicked into place for K.O. Alani was off the hook in her mind; however, that wasn't good enough.

"What was all that about 'the stakes being high,' and *Ka Leo's* getting too radical, and can't you do something?'"

"I just meant that I understood that if we want our culture to be recognized and respected, we have to give of ourselves. Our time, our money. Like I said, if we have to raise people's conciousness by public rallies, and maybe going to jail, that's all part of it."

He sighed again. "But when it turns to people getting killed, or even hurt, well, how are we better than what happened during the overthrow? We should be better than that. Otherwise, what have we learned? Where did we grow?"

K.O. digested that for a moment. "I have another question."

"Okay." Alani seemed subdued, and a little surprised at the change in her manner. "Go ahead."

"The chisel they found at the scene matches the chisel you use, right?"

"Yes."

"Are you sure it was yours?"

"Sure. I mean, I guess so. It looked like mine. What are you getting at?"

"Yours is missing, and an identical one turns up at the crime scene, right?"

"Yeah?"

"Okay, you were covered with blood from cutting yourself on

the chisel, right?"

"Well, not that chisel, but yeah."

"What do you mean, not that chisel?"

"I wasn't using that one. I haven't used it for a couple weeks."

"What?"

"I had not used that chisel in a couple weeks. I couldn't find it. I cut myself on a different chisel," Alani repeated slowly.

"And the chisel they found at the scene matched the chisel you lost?"

"Yes, I think it was mine."

K.O. racked her brain. All the tools in Alani's workshop had been impounded at the time of his arrest, so there were other tools in evidence. She had focused on the one that matched Mr. Kaneali'ihiwi's. Nothing else made sense. That had to be a piece of the puzzle. If it wasn't, well . . . that would make her crazy.

"Did you explain about your chisel being lost?"

"Explain?"

"To Homicide!"

"Sure, but they didn't believe me. Besides, the one they found is mine."

"Are you sure? This is important!"

"I think I'm sure."

"So it's possible it isn't?"

"I suppose there's a slim chance, but K.O., why? Besides, it's an antique, one of a kind. You can't go to the hardware store and buy that."

"Where did you get yours?"

"My wood-carving mentor gave it to me years ago."

"Would that person be the senior Kaneali'ihiwi of the Hawaiian Homelands eviction case?"

K.O. heard an intake of breath. "Yes. How do you know?"

"I paid him a little visit this morning. He was carving Ku. With a chisel that identically matched the one in my evidence locker."

"Ku?"

"Stick to the point! Did you know he had a second chisel?"

A pause. "I don't think so. I haven't worked with him in years. The only time I've seen him recently is in connection with the eviction."

"Could there be a third chisel?"

"I don't know."

"Is it possible?"

"Yes," Alani said slowly. "Sometimes tools were made in sets. "

"Who else would know about your chisel? These chisels. Besides Kumu."

Alani paused. "Not too many people, I guess. Maybe other woodworkers? K.O., I just don't know. This is a lot to process."

"I know. I'm thinking of this case in a whole different way. I figured out the Homelands issue was in the middle of it, and now I think the Kanealiʻihiwis are in the middle of that. I just don't know how."

"You don't think Kumu Kanealiʻihiwi is responsible for a murder, do you?" Disbelief echoed over the phone.

"No. Not really. But he's connected somehow. I think he knows who is—or at least suspects. He said it was personal, and committed by a Hawaiian."

"He said that?"

"Not in so many words. But 'personal' could still mean the Hawaiian lands, because that's hugely personal to so many."

"Yes, it is."

"Could someone feel threatened by your woodworking ability?"

"What do you mean?"

"You know, jealous, maybe? A competitor? Would someone want to frame you, to get you out of the business?"

Alani sounded startled. "I wouldn't have thought so, but I guess at this stage, I can't rule anything out. Can I?" His tone was pointed, and she worked not to squirm.

"Think about it. See if anyone comes to mind, okay?"

K.O. had just thought of someone else she wanted to talk to. Donna Costello at the Honolulu Medical Examiner's Office. "Look, Alani, I gotta go."

"K.O. I'm really sorry. About us. I do care for you. About you."

Just what K.O. wanted to hear. Not love, not that love was even a possibility. *Shit.* "Okay, Alani. I know. I'm sorry about sort of, pointing Homicide at you. I didn't mean for you to get arrested."

"What did you think would happen?" He didn't sound mad, just sad.

"I don't know. Do me—well, both of us, a favor. Don't say anything about my third-chisel theory to anyone, okay? I gotta check out a few more things. You are not going to go down for this."

"Tell my lawyer. He's preparing my defense, and I look guilty even to me."

"Alani, don't. Maybe when this is over, we'll still be friends at the other end, but I *am* trying to help you now."

"Okay. I guess I know that. It's hard to wait for a bunch of people to decide your future. Jail or freedom. And for what? I was just trying to help Mr. Kanealiʻihiwi."

"Yeah, but any association you have with Nahua is going to come out in court, sooner or later."

"Thanks for the vote of confidence."

"I'm just saying, Nahua is in some bad shit, Federal shit, and you don't want to be near him. Talk about that with your lawyer."

"Right. Let me know how my life is going, okay?"

"I will. Bye." K.O. hung up sad and discouraged. Now she knew. She and Alani were nada, zip, zilch, over.

"I guess it's better to find out now, rather than after we're married with two kids."

She grabbed her purse and left the office, barely holding back more tears.

"What a wuss." She had never realized how much she had

thought Alani was "the one," until he so wasn't. "At least I can cry over it with Donna and six beers," she mumbled.

But where she ended up was George's house.

CHAPTER THIRTY-ONE

Poor George defenselessly opened the door to a wet, weepy K.O. who had nothing more to offer than an opened bag of mac nuts stashed in her purse.

"Hi, Scarlet. Tough day at the office?"

Her stream of tears turned into Hurricane Iwa. George guided her inside his cozy house and plopped her onto the sofa, covered her with a blankie, and set a highball glass of bourbon and Diet Pepsi within reach.

"Tell Rhett all about it." He slung an arm around her shoulders and slurped noisily from his own glass, thus encouraging her to do the same. She did.

"Ah, shit, George. Why didn't you marry me?"

"Well. Let's see. We didn't love each other like that, and meaningless sex seemed . . . well, so meaningless." He slurped again. "Besides. We are much better off as friends. See? If we were ex-lovers, where would you be right now? On a small sofa in a total stranger's house, begging for bourbon and Diet Pepsi, which no stranger in his right mind would supply. That's something only friends do."

K.O. eyed him, unsure where his gentle teasing left off.

"Come on, Scarlet. Who's Your Daddy?"

K.O. snorted an unladylike honk of genuine laughter. "Let me lay this out, and you tell me what to do, okay?"

"Okay. First, refill." He did and settled this time in his recliner, a sure sign of complete attention.

"I've found out a number of things, some of which are germaine to the case. Others are merely depressing."

"Where do you want to start? Germaine, or depressing?"

"You're so funny, Rhett. Remind me to burn Tara again when I've gotten all the use out of you I can."

"Right. Duly noted. Let's start with depressing."

"Great. Brilliant." K.O. told him about Alani. How their relationship had been pretty much in her head. "I need a guy's opinion." She opened her hands and thrust them at George. "I don't get it. He gave me signs! Wine, homemade dinner, flowers, rain. A card. I thought it was gonna be the night, you know?"

"What night?"

"Aw, come on, George, the night. Has it been that long for you?"

"No." He looked smug. "I just can't believe it's been that long for you."

"Ha, ha. You are so funny. I just thought we had something special."

"You did. You do. You just pushed him into a corner—like you do, I might add—and he panicked. He couldn't say what he thought. What he wanted."

"Why not?"

"I don't know. Some guys can." He looked deeply inside his glass and shrugged.

"George? George! You are one of those guys! We have never been involved romantically, so I never would have guessed. Well." K.O. took a long, noisy slurp. "Whaddya know? This calls for a refill. Then I'll tell you about the German parts." She held out her glass.

"Do you mean, germaine?" George took the glass and went back to the kitchen.

"Whatever. Just bring the damn bottle back with you, dude, 'kay?"

"Whatever," came from the kitchen. George reappeared with the bottle as instructed, ice, and the remains of the Diet Pepsi bottle. "Ick." He set the soda down as if it were slime-covered.

Briefly, K.O. thought of the consequences of drinking too much. Briefly. That soon went away, however, and she related as much as she could piece together of the case. Sometime later, she realized she'd been there for several hours.

"George? Um, do you have plans tonight?"

"Yup."

"Should I go and let you get to it?"

"Nope. I canceled. No way you're going home in your condition. Besides, I'm in no condition for a date, so there."

"Thanks, George. What do you think?" At his lack of response she added, "Of the case?"

"Oh. That. I think you're on the right track. You have the pieces. Now you have the murder weapon and a theory about that. The middle is the Homelands issue and the Kaneali'ihiwi homestead. Go back. Talk to the wood-carver. He has more to say. Ask about the chisel. Get inside his house. He's not necessarily hiding anything, but something is there for you to find."

"I was beginning to think that, too." K.O. pushed the blanket off her and rose unsteadily. "Bathroom, first—sleep, next." She walked to the doorway. "I needed to go back there, but I needed you to tell me. I didn't want to go. It's creepy. But I will. Thanks again, George."

When K.O. returned to her couch, George had gone. To his bed, she assumed.

She downed a huge glass of water and got another for the evening, attempting to dilute what promised to be a huge hangover.

Only what I deserve, she thought. "Now, for hallucinogenic, if not prophetic dreams." She dropped into fitful, but immediate sleep, feeling safe as always, in George's care.

CHAPTER THIRTY-TWO

As she predicted, K.O. woke up with a hangover. Not too bad as hangovers went, but enough to make her move delicately to the bathroom, then to the kitchen. George looked the way she felt, dragged "back asswards" through a knothole.

"Hey," said K.O.

"Didja get the license number of that truck that hit us?" George shoved a mug of coffee at her.

"No, I missed that in the train wreck." She smiled weakly and took a hit of coffee. George scooted a bottle of ibuprophen across the table. K.O. shook out two and downed them with another slurp.

"Hungry?" George asked.

"Ugh."

"Good. Eat a bagel, it'll help."

K.O. noticed several bagel slices next to the toaster along with butter and cream cheese. She reached over and slid an "everything" slice into the slot, wincing at the clang of the toaster.

"What are you doing today," George asked. "Nap?"

"No. I have to pay for my sins by doing something constructive. I'm going to talk to Donna, which I had meant to do, and should have done last night." She tried to look ferocious.

"If she's any kind of friend at all, you'd still look and feel like this today."

"Yeah. Probably." The toaster popped, and K.O. buttered and cream-cheesed her slice. It smelled good, and she took a tentative bite. It seemed to stay where it was supposed to, so she took another. "What are you going to do today?"

"I'm going to have a nap and then make amends for the last minute cancellation from last night."

"Oh, yeah. I'm sorry, George."

"That's all right. Making up is sort of fun, if you do it right." He winked.

"You really are a rascal, you know?"

"Yeah." He smiled. "Seriously, regarding the evidence you mentioned. Call me if you have questions. You want this to stick in court, and from what you said, no one else knows about the antique chisel set, except maybe the murderer. Be careful."

"I always am, George."

"I bet." They finished their bagels and coffee, and K.O. headed home to change and reconnoiter.

As always, coming home to her condo on the windward side felt so peaceful. Teresa's strident yowling and litany of complaints somewhat diminished the peace, but K.O. had to admit Teresa had a point.

After taking a hot shower and drinking a gallon of water while cuddling Teresa in the recliner, K.O. felt somewhat restored.

She called the Medical Examiner's Office to find that Donna had taken the day off.

"Crap." She tried Donna at home, but her machine picked up. "Hey, Donna, it's K.O. Give me a call. I want to go over those stupid cases again. I have a theory I want to run by you. I'm at home now, but will probably run out to the homestead again later this afternoon. I'm off today and don't expect to be in the office."

She disconnected, and realized that although her house really needed attention, as did Teresa, what she really should do was visit Richard and Abby one last time before they took off for home.

She called the hospital and learned they had been released. "I wonder why they didn't call me to help them?" She dialed the hotel.

Richard answered, and K.O. asked if she could take them to the airport or help with their packing.

"That's real nice of you, Katrina." Richard repeated what she had said to Abby, who was somewhere in the room.

A thump and a rustling, and Abby spoke. "We leave in about fifteen minutes, dear."

"What? Why didn't you tell me?"

"You've done so much already. We didn't want to bother you."

"Bother me? Of course I want to take you to the airport. When's your flight?" K.O. knew she could not make it from Kaneohe to Waikiki in fifteen minutes. She also knew if she didn't make a miracle and take them to the airport herself, her mother would kill her, and then make the rest of her life miserable. That was all she needed.

"When is our flight, dear?" Abby asked Richard.

A pause, then she said, "Katrina? Our plane leaves at 3:15."

"It's only noon. I can be there in thirty minutes." *I hope.*

"Oh. Richard? What do you think?" K.O. heard Abby's voice fade as she repeated the whole thing. Then she returned. "Why, thank you dear. Richard says we'll meet you in thirty minutes then." The phone went dead.

"Oh, shit!" K.O. flew around her condo, grabbing purse, clean T-shirt, sandals, water. She dumped kibble in Teresa's bowl, while Teresa refused to meet her eye. "Sorry, sorry!" K.O. was out the door in under five minutes.

She chose the Pali Highway and prayed for no traffic at this midday hour. There was a little slowing, but it wasn't bad. She made it to the front of their hotel in thirty-five minutes, but the elevator seemed to add five more.

Abby answered the door. The luggage was open and garments and sundries had spilled onto the rug. A trail of shoes, vials, paperbacks, and other items led from room to room as if they had dropped them en route from storage to suitcase.

"Ready to go?" K.O. asked brightly as she looked despairingly around. How could they have gotten to the airport without assistance? she wondered.

"Almost," Richard said from where he sat in the recliner.

"Okay. Let's get this closed up and loaded. Where are your carry-ons? I'll make sure your books and meds are in there."

"Oh, here." Abby waved vaguely, and K.O. saw her purse and a small canvas bag imprinted with Air Canada. She began to sweat as she gathered items. The minutes ticked by as she folded, packed, zipped, and consoled.

"Where are the tickets?" K.O. surveyed the room with a bit of relief, now that everything seemed to be contained.

"Tickets?" Abby repeated.

Oh, my God, thought K.O., *not this too.*

"Right here in my pocket," Richard said, patting his coat.

"Let's just make sure of the times, okay?" K.O. prayed that all was well and kicked herself for checking this last instead of first. The gods were with them, though. The tickets were in order.

A blur of time while she got them downstairs—into the car, luggage loaded—and raced down Nimitz Highway. The agricultural inspection and airline check-in; wheelchairs for two to the gate. Negotiation for wheelchairs in Seattle. *Thank God for a direct flight from Honolulu.*

She waited until the plane taxied away from the gate before she gave into her exhaustion and sat, breathing as if she'd run in the Ironman. She bought a large bottle of water and popped two more ibuprophen, then made her way slowly out of the congested airport and onto the freeway.

It was after four when she got home. Her night of bourbon caught up with her, and she lay in bed, with Teresa on the pillow next to her, and fell into an exhausted sleep.

She woke the next morning, surprised at how long she'd slept. It was early. What had awakened her was the phone ringing.

"Hello?" she said groggily.

"K.O.? It's Ben."

At first, K.O. didn't recognize the name or the voice. "Ben?"

"Donna's assistant."

Tiny. "Oh, yeah. Howzit?"

"Not good. I think we have a problem. Can we meet?"

"Sure, I'll come to the office."

"No. Not here. Donna asked me to call for her because she's found something and she wants to talk to you privately."

"Sure, Tiny, no prob. Where and when?"

"It's Ben."

"Ben."

"Can you meet at the homestead tonight?"

"The homestead?"

"The Kaneali'ihiwis'. Six o'clock."

"Okay. Sure. Is Donna in the office yet?" She squinted at the clock. It wasn't unusual for Donna to be in the office before eight.

"No. She took the day off."

"She took yesterday off, too. Is she sick?" Donna never took days off. Except the time she was bitten by a centipede that was lurking in the bottom of her gardening glove. Her arm had swollen up and she'd had difficulty breathing. She'd gone to the hospital where the staff had been so excited to see her they'd nearly forgotten about treating her bite.

"No. She's fine. What do you want to talk to her about?"

He seemed sort of short with her, but maybe he wasn't an early morning person like his boss. "Nothing that important. I'll wait until tonight. It'll keep."

K.O. wanted to talk to White Collar Crimes again anyway. See if they could fill her in on Kepa Nahua and *Ka Leo* versus the HCS. Lots to keep her busy today.

"See you tonight. Don't forget, six o'clock."
"Bye, Tiny. I mean, Ben."
K.O. hung up and stretched, ready to start her day.

CHAPTER THIRTY-THREE

As K.O. made coffee, she realized she had passed over something that could be important. She had never gone back and reviewed or researched the Ellis file. She couldn't get access to that crime scene in the cave, but she had also neglected to review Richards's file thoroughly, and she could certainly get into that crime scene.

She called Homicide. "Hey, Roly, it's K.O. What are you doing in? Aren't you three to eleven?"

"Why? You calling now to avoid me?"

She laughed. "Nah, actually, you're the best guy to talk to."

"Lucky me. What's up?"

"Couple things. Did you guys ever close off Ellis's residence as part of the investigation?"

"Jeez, K.O.! Let it alone already. I told you, we're handling it. Stay out."

"Come on, Roly. I might have something, here."

"If you *'have something here,'* you should give it to me."

"Well, not something-something. Nothing sure, I mean. Come on, please? Just a couple questions and I'll be gone."

"Shit. Okay. We closed off the residence, his place in Kahala.

But the family is back there now. Before you ask, we didn't find anything useful. He wasn't killed at home, and he didn't have any files, computers, whatevers, that would help us. Satisfied?"

"Okay, thanks. What about Richards's place?"

"What about it?"

"Is it still closed?"

"Yes. It's a crime scene."

"Can I get in there?"

"What?"

"I need to see it. Please?"

"K.O. you are one pushy b—"

"Roly!"

"Broad! I was going to say broad."

"Right. Take me there, Roly. I've got a hunch. You must have fifteen minutes of your day I can borrow?"

"Borrow? That's good." K.O. heard his chair squeak and knew he was leaning back, weighing giving into her and getting her off his back—temporarily at least—against following procedure to the letter.

"Okay, you win." Roly sighed heavily. "I can meet you tomorrow—"

"Tomorrow, no! I need to go today."

"You don't want much, do you?"

"I'll buy you lunch. Anything, Roly, please."

"All right already. Meet me at the station at eleven. I'll take you over and then you buying me lunch. Two."

"Thanks, Roly! That's great. I'll be good, I promise. Any chance of you introducing me to the Ellis family so I can look around their place?"

"No!"

"Okay. Just asking." But K.O. was jubilant. Getting into Richards's apartment was a big deal, and K.O. knew the risk Roly was taking. Of course Homicide was finished there, had been done hours after the discovery, but they liked to hang on to a hot scene as long as possible.

She hurriedly dressed and grabbed some toast, threw together what she thought she'd need for the day, squeezed Teresa good-bye, and flew out the door.

Traffic was light, and she made it to the station in plenty of time. She called Donna's home number from her desk.

Still no answer, just the machine.

She left another message. What she really wanted to do was bounce ideas off Donna, and review her crime scene and death investigation reports. Her friend had a good eye and was a thorough investigator.

K.O. sat back and thought. If she reviewed Ellis's reports, viewed Richards's apartment, bought Roly lunch, maybe she'd have time for a quick visit to the Medical Examiner's Office. Then she and Donna could ride together to the Kaneali'ihiwis' place.

If Donna wasn't available, the next best thing was Donna's work. Maybe Tiny—well, Ben—was working and could help her get into the computer to see the photos and reports. She could still make it to the homestead by six to meet Donna. Whatever *that* was about. It would kill two birds with one stone, however, because she had wanted to talk to Mr. Kaneali'ihiwi again about that chisel theory.

"Okee doke." K.O. pushed back from her desk and gathered up her omnipresent files on the most important case, which wasn't hers. Not only was the case not hers, but she could get in deep shit for what "they" might term interfering with an investigation.

In Homicide, Roly was working on a report in his cubicle.

"Hi, Roly. Ready for lunch?" K.O. leaned on the partition that made up the entrance.

"Sure. One sec." Roly looked up an address, filled it in, and set the report aside. "Let's go."

By silent assent, they didn't talk until they were in Roly's official vehicle and pulling out of the HPD garage.

"Thanks again, Roly."

"This is a one-time deal. And no touching, no moving, no breathing. Got it?"

"Got it."

The short drive to the Kinau street apartment filled K.O. with anxiety. They could both get into trouble for this. Serious trouble. What right did she have to ask this of Roly? She took a deep breath and exhaled.

They climbed the two sets of stairs to the third-floor cinder-block apartment. The building itself was a U-shaped three-story, the pool in the center. Wooden louvres in all the windows let in air but not much light. Most apartments had not only the windows open, but the front doors as well, to take advantage of any breeze in humid Honolulu.

Richards's apartment was closed up and dark. Police tape zigged across the door. The smell of old blood had faded some, but still leaked from the closed louvres.

Roly popped the tape and inserted a key. With the door open, the odor rolled out and covered them in its acrid stench.

"Walk where I walk." Roly led the way.

K.O. trod softly in his wake. The narrow front hall was tiled in inexpensive vinyl squares of a brown, green, and orange design. It took K.O. a moment to realize that some of the design was spattered blood.

A thin trail of it began several feet back from the door, where the front hall met the living room. A rust-brown lake covered several feet of green shag carpet.

"He was first hit here." Roly pointed to the first spatter, near the hall and living room juncture. "It split him open, but he was a big guy and strong, and didn't go down. He knew the assailant and let him in, probably voluntarily. When he turned to lead him into the living room, he got the first hit on the head. Maybe the killer was surprised when he didn't drop then, but Richards managed to stagger into the living room before he fell. He was alive when the stabbing started."

"Did you find the object he was hit with first?"

"Yeah, a chunk of *'a'a* lava. Didn't hold prints. Still, grains embedded in the skull. He wasn't beaten though. That was just to knock him out. He died of multiple stab wounds. Took a while to die."

K.O. saw a smaller, smudged trail of blood leave the main area. "What's that?"

"Where the guy went to the bathroom and washed up. Nothing useful really. Pulled the drains, etc., but other than a few hairs which turned out to be Richards's, we only got blood and regular drain crap."

She remembered Richards's long, wavy hair, and was saddened again. She recalled her fear at his size and power, and knew he probably hadn't been the world's best citizen, but she didn't like the thought of him murdered this way. The assailant had wanted him to suffer, had drawn out the crime so he would. A chill ran down her spine at the addition of this sinister element.

"We got footprints in the blood, see?" He pointed to the ovoid patterns in the carpet.

"If you say so." They looked like most of the other blobs to K.O.

"But by the time he hits the tile in the bathroom, not enough to use."

She was beginning to feel a little nauseated from the sheer amount of blood and the atmosphere of violence that remained in the apartment. Finally, she was able to tear her eyes away from the floors and glance around at the home.

"Can we walk around a little?"

"Follow me exactly." Roly led her around the perimeter, pointing out additional spatter, the location of the weapons, and where Homicide had removed evidence.

K.O. saw, from the decor, that Blala had supported local artists, because his walls, shelves, and tables displayed a remarkable collection of art and artifacts. A variety of vintage ukuleles hung on the walls, and she was impressed with the number and variety of books on his shelves. She felt invasive, as if there had been much more to this powerful man than he had wanted the world to see.

She was about to tell Roly she was ready to go when she noticed the photographs hanging on the wall.

Framed photos hung in a montage in the short hall to the bathroom. She had been so caught up in the physical scene that she had barely lifted her head past the spattered floor.

"Roly. Do you know this guy?" K.O. pointed to a photo of three very young men: Blala Richards, Kepa Nahua, and a third man, their arms slung over each other's shoulders, Corona beers in hand, leaning sloppily against palm trees.

"He looks familiar, but I can't place him."

K.O.'s stomach lurched, and despite the age of the photo, she knew exactly who the third man was. It could be a coincidence, but she didn't think so.

It would explain so much. How the assailant had such vast knowledge and how he had achieved the crimes with such apparent ease.

What she didn't have was motive.

She almost blurted her discovery to Roly, but then she remembered what had happened the last time she'd pointed out a connection to him. She had told him about Alani's conversation with Nahua, and he'd arrested Alani for murder.

What if there was an innocent explanation for this photo? She doubted there was, but this time she had to make sure first.

"Can I have this?" K.O. indicated the photo.

"No, you can't have this." Roly shook his head. "Who is it?"

"Give me one day, and I'll tell you."

"K.O., I can take it into evidence myself and ID it that way."

"I know, I know! But just give me the rest of today, and I promise, you'll get the whole thing with a ribbon, and you'll be famous."

"Yeah, famous," Roly grumbled as they backtracked out of the apartment. "Notorious and arrested, more like. Al Capone was famous. Charles Manson was famous." He locked the door. "You'd better call me before the end of my regular shift. Eleven o'clock tonight. That's it. Then I'm covering my own ass by taking yours down."

"Okay, Roly. Thanks."

The few blocks ride back to the station to her own car took forever, but K.O.'s brain clicked rapidly. So much fell into place if she was right. But she couldn't do to another person what she had done to Alani: accuse without evidence. She had to know for sure. If she did it wrong, more than one career would tank.

She abstractedly thanked Roly and got into her car, heading for the Medical Examiner's Office and Donna's computer.

And some answers, she hoped.

CHAPTER THIRTY-FOUR

K.O. parked in the Medical Examiner's lot on Iwilei street. A lab tech buzzed her through the locked front door. The chemical smell hit her, but not with its usual intensity.

"I must be getting used to this," she grumbled as she headed upstairs to Donna's office.

The maze of offices was quiet. She poked her head into the main room where a number of desks sat. Empty. She went to the lab, but that was empty too. Even the tech who'd let her in had disappeared.

"Maybe they're all downstairs on a case." She stood in the doorway to Donna's office, hands on hips. She didn't want to bother the staff if they were doing an autopsy, but she didn't really want to get caught rummaging around Donna's office either.

She knew Donna wouldn't mind—would trust her not to take advantage and poke into things that were none of her business—but still . . . .

K.O. didn't know how long she'd have to wait to ask. It was nearing four o'clock. Some of the employees would be taking off for the day. The M.E.'s office was a 24/7 kind of job, but most of the staff kept shift hours.

What to do?

With her usual determination, K.O. closed the front door to Donna's office to avoid the casual glance and interrogation by a passerby. She left the back door ajar, nervous now.

If she needed help, there was no one around. Why would she need help? *Stupid,* she chided herself. She sat at Donna's desk and exhaled, her nerves calming with the task at hand.

She systematically checked the piled desktop for the files and was not surprised when she couldn't find anything related to these cases.

"Probably took them home to work on."

Next she turned her attention to the computer. She had known Donna's password once, and hoped it hadn't changed. When she jigged the mouse, the screensaver cleared and the password window opened. She typed in "707gsw." The penal code pre-fix for homicide, followed by the abbreviation for gunshot wound.

The main menu popped up. She chose the search option and was rewarded when the correct cases appeared. She was unfamiliar with the software Donna used and could not figure out how she had made more than one case come up simultaneously for comparison, so she had to flip back and forth between the two cases by clicking on the tabs at the bottom of the screen.

She didn't find anything she'd overlooked until she got to the bottom of the last screen, where the reports were printed and signed by the investigator or investigators.

On the bottom of the Ellis case, signature spaces had been left for both Donna and Tiny, and on the Richards case, only Donna's name had a space. She knew they each filed a separate report, but also that Donna reviewed them as the supervisor. Had Tiny assisted on that case? She sat back from the computer and thought. Was there a way to find out without asking Donna before tonight?

From the ideas session she, Donna, and Tiny had had in this office, she'd gotten the impression that he was at the scene, too. She could confirm this if she found the paper copy of the report.

Maybe this was an unfinished version of the report.

She pulled a file off the pile on the desk and flipped to the end to look for signatures. She continued through the stack of manila folders, comparing.

In the majority of cases, Tiny had investigated, too. He had filed his own report, signed it, and then Donna had signed as well.

K.O. opened the last file and another report, not fixed into the folder like the others, slithered out.

She saw it was an original version of the autopsy on Ellis. Odd. Why would that be here? Not even in the correct folder with the rest of the Ellis homicide reports? Donna might appear disorganzied since her office was somewhat of a wreck, but that was a misperception.

Not an accident, then. Donna must have hidden this.

K.O. carefully read each line and box. She nearly crowed when she found it. What had been bothering her about the other reports, the crime scene data, all of it. Even as she felt elated, she knew why Donna had hidden it. Her own suspicions confirmed. Time. It was all about time. Ellis's time of death had been altered on subsequent reports. The change meant the murderer now had an alibi. Probably an official alibi—an unbreakable, unimpeachable alibi. Brilliant. She hid the report again. If it hadn't been found so far, that was good enough. She'd promised Roly evidence. Well, now she had it.

She glanced at her watch, and gasped. It was five. She had to get going to the homestead to meet Donna. She would be late, and even later if traffic was heavy. So, Roly would have to wait a bit.

She closed out the files on the computer, straightened the stacks of files she'd disturbed, and poked her head out the door.

She could hear distant voices in conversation. Coming from the lab? She hoped so. She didn't want to be caught leaving.

She didn't know why, but the nerves were back, and she just wanted out. The chill air, the wafting chemicals, the oppressive atmosphere made her tiptoe quickly down the stairs and out into the heat and pollution of Iwilei. She didn't feel comfortable until she was driving west on Nimitz Highway, happily trapped in the everyday grind of an evening's commute. It felt almost normal.

CHAPTER THIRTY-FIVE

K.O. arrived at the Kanealiʻihiwi homestead just after six. Darkness fell earlier on this side of the Koʻolau mountains, and the house sat amid lush foliage like a large gray spider, silent and ominous in its web.

She saw no vehicles, and thought it odd she'd beaten Donna there, given Donna's penchant for punctuality and dedication to her work.

What could Donna want to make her choose to meet out here? It had to be something with the murders, but why here?

A sudden chill ran up K.O.'s spine. She felt very exposed sitting in her car in the front yard. The house looked much the same as the last time she'd been here, but the approaching gloom made it seem even more sinister. No breeze stirred the curtains, and the palm trunk carving was absent from the front porch.

She saw tire tracks leading around behind the house, and followed them on foot to find an old, narrow garage, separate from the house. It appeared to be a former carriage house and now held a car unfamiliar to K.O.

Hmmm, she thought. *I guess that's enough snooping for now.* She supposed the poor man was entitled to park his car anywhere he wanted on his own property.

She made her way back to the front. For a house that was supposed to be occupied, it had the most unoccupied feeling.

As she approached the door, the porch squeaked. She stopped and listened. In the silence she could hear the distant crash of waves from the bay, but no birds, no traffic, no rustlings or scuttlings of rodents or mongoose.

She strained to hear something from inside the house. On one level, she knew she was being ridiculous, catering to her nerves. If she had been at an apartment or house in town, she might have approached with caution, but not this sort of stalking-cat wariness.

On the other hand, better to look stupid than to make a mistake. And, though she heard no sounds from within, she felt a sense of waiting and watching.

Oh, for Pete's sake. If Mr. Kaneali'ihiwi is in there, and he and Donna are waiting for me, having tea or something, they must be wondering what the hell my problem is.

She knocked.

The door was opened almost immediately, and by the last person she had expected, the man from the photograph in Blala Richards's apartment.

"K.O. So glad you could make it. Come on in," Ben Sugano said.

"Hey, Ben. How are you?" She strove for a casual tone, but felt she failed. "What are you doing here?" She entered warily.

"Donna knows I'm familiar with the cases." He turned from the door and let her shut it as he led the way deeper into the house.

He hadn't answered the question, but K.O. stayed close as he passed through the living room and headed down a darkened hall to a lighter kitchen in the back.

What she saw in the kitchen made her freeze—long enough for Ben to produce a gun and point it at her chest.

Donna sat in a straight-backed chair at the kitchen table, a cup of steaming tea in front of her, just as K.O. had pictured. Almost. What she hadn't pictured, was that Donna would be bound hand and foot to that straight-backed chair.

"K.O."

Donna's voice was raspy, and for an instant K.O. wondered two things—why she hadn't been gagged, and why her voice was strange. Then while Ben looked on like a proud daddy, she answered both herself. Donna hadn't been gagged because there was no need. Out here in the middle of nowhere, no one could hear her scream. And that seemed to be what she had done. Screamed until her voice was gone.

Judging from Ben's expression, he had enjoyed every minute of it.

"Where is Mr. Kaneali'ihiwi? Have you hurt him?" K.O. demanded.

"He is away for a few days."

"Away as in a trip, or did you do something to him?" K.O. insisted.

"I would never hurt Grandfather." Ben looked shocked at the idea.

Then it registered. "He's your grandfather?" Now things made sense.

She turned to Donna. "Has he hurt you?" She stepped towards her friend.

"Uh, uh, uh," Ben said, wagging his finger the way he might to a misbehaving toddler. "Don't move any closer."

K.O. stopped. Her brain bounced back and forth between questions and answers. Standing between Donna and Ben, she asked him, "Why did you take Donna?"

"Oh, I think she might know the answer to that. But let's be comfortable. Sit." He gestured to a chair across the table and far from them both. K.O. sat. "I think you should be restrained a bit, too."

Her heart sank as she saw him yank a roll of duct tape from

his pocket. She had seen Donna's red and swollen wrists and wondered if she'd been here, tied for the two days she'd not been in the office.

Anger swelled inside her, but she kept her face neutral.

"Put your purse on the table. Slowly."

K.O. complied. Ben threw it on the kitchen counter several feet away. "Put your hands behind your back."

The blow was glancing but unexpected when he punched her head from behind. "Behind the chair! Don't play games with me."

She arranged her arms as her vision swam.

She tried to lock eyes with Donna, to tell her it would be okay. She wasn't sure how it would be, though. Donna's eyes were huge and fear-filled. K.O. could not tell how much she was processing. It would be helpful if they could hatch a plot together, but if Donna was injured, in shock, or had just left the planet, K.O. would be on her own.

Ben secured her wrists to his satisfaction, then ran his hands around her waist and frisked her from foot to knee.

"Can't be too careful with you, can I, K.O.? I've heard what a pitbull you can be." He settled himself in a third kitchen chair and put the gun on the table, tantalizingly close. Then he laced his hands behind his head and leaned back, looking for all the world as if they might discuss the rise in taxes or how outrageous the price of a gallon of milk was at Foodland.

Even sitting, Ben was a large man, and K.O. could see how he might have overpowered a man like Blala Richards if he was caught off guard.

Gee, and speaking of being caught off guard, K.O. thought bitterly.

"Well, Donna—*Boss*—let's hear from you. Why are you here?"

Donna cleared her throat, clearly frightened. "I made a mistake."

"That's right. You did. And what was that mistake?"

"I was too nosy."

"Yes, you were. What did you learn?"

"You are the grandson and first heir of the Kanealiʻihiwi family."

"He is?" K.O. blurted. "How did you find that out?"

Donna glanced at Ben, who nodded. "I noticed a discrepancy on the original Ellis autopsy report. The time of death had been changed. Ben was the only one who could have changed that. It made me think I was missing something else, so I looked up his original personnel file." Her voice seemed to lose force, but she struggled on. "It showed his full name, Ben Kanealiʻihiwi Sugano. The homestead eviction has been on the front page all week. You and I have talked so much about Alani and these cases that I knew it was not a coincidence. I found that he's a direct descendant and heir."

Ben beamed. "What's a little rearranging of evidence and report tampering among friends? Go on." That was to Donna.

"Can I have a drink? Please?" Donna whispered.

Impatiently, Ben leaned over and picked up the tea mug and gave her a sip. Donna's lips pulled at the liquid, but he removed the cup. "Now, now. Save some for later."

Donna licked her lips and swallowed.

K.O.'s hands clenched behind her back. She felt the tape pull at the hair and skin at her wrists. She wanted to rip Ben apart, but she would have to rip the tape first to do it.

Donna continued. "Ellis was the driving force behind the homestead eviction. Because Ben was an heir, he was privy to all the family information, and because he was an investigator with me, he was privy to most of the criminal information, too"

"So, I stayed one step ahead of all of you." He smiled. "Until you. Until now." He looked at Donna, then at K.O.

K.O.'s brain raced. *Keep him talking, keep him calm.* "No wonder we had such a tough time. I knew I was missing something. I kept getting mixed up with the *Ka Leo* thing."

"Of course you would be mixed up. What about *Ka Leo? It* was only a matter of time before my true potential was recognized there as well."

Now K.O. was truly confused. Discovering that Ben was the heir to the homestead lands was news that explained a lot, but it didn't explain *Ka Leo,* Richards's murder, or Alani's involvement.

She looked at Ben's hands as they toyed with the gun. Big, strong hands. A lot like Alani's. Since he was in the photo with Nahua and Richards, since he knew them and was the heir to the Homelands estate, and the grandson of a wood-carver, then it wasn't too far a reach for him to have committed a second murder. And if he had committed two, what were two more?

As K.O. contemplated how to extract more information and buy time, Ben pushed himself back from the table. "I want to show you two ladies something." He left the kitchen and returned immediately with a chisel. A chisel K.O. knew well, and had seen many times before. Ben threw the chisel on the table between them. "What do you think of that? I'm going to show you what that beauty can do."

Her heart hammering, K.O. met his gaze, and Donna burst into tears, while the chisel gently rocked back and forth.

CHAPTER THIRTY-SIX

K.O. watched the chisel rock seductively on the kitchen table at the Kanealiʻihiwi house. Her palms became slick when she thought of what this man had already done with a similar instrument. She would try to play it cool. She refused to look at Donna who had begun to cry again—Donna, who had intimate knowledge of what that chisel had done.

"Nice tool. Yours?" K.O. asked.

"Yes. A gift from Grandfather. Part of a set as I'm sure you know." Ben stood calmly now, his dark hair like a helmet in the kitchen light.

Why didn't I notice he's built like a wrestler? K.O. wondered. His T-shirt revealed ropes of muscle previously hidden by loose Aloha shirts. "I understand that you wanted to stop Ellis from moving the eviction ahead, so you killed him. But he's a government guy. They're just going to replace him, right?"

"Not right away. It's become so political, it's only helped fuel the fire of our cause. Besides, it buys me time to come up with another plan."

"Okay, so what does the golf course thing have to do with this? I mean Ellis and the golf course?" K.O. stalled.

"Nothing really. Just a happy coincidence that Ellis was dirty. He was on the take from the consortium to buy land any way they could get it. He was in a position of power both with information and the ability to persuade the 'right' committees. A word here, a buck there." Ben set the chisel to rocking again.

"Your grandfather told me the consortium could never own these particular lands. Is that true?"

"Yes. They are protected through the royal line in perpetuity."

"Then how did the golf course and your grandfather's eviction become combined?"

"An anonymous tip here and there." His eyes twinkled with pride. "It didn't take much at all to get everyone all *huhu* about it,. Certain people only see what they want to see," he gave K.O. and Donna a hard look. "And are only too willing to believe what's right in front of them."

So true. K.O. squirmed at how quickly she'd turned Alani in.

"It just seemed to serve a greater good to take care of Ellis. Solved a lot of problems." He looked at her speculatively. "Seems I have a couple more I need to take care of."

Donna sniffed. *Great. He'll kill someone just to buy time. Not even a permanent solution. A stop-gap measure. Shit.*

"When I was at Richards's house, I saw a photo of you with Kepa Nahua and Blala Richards. You obviously knew them both. Why would you kill Richards? After what you've just said, he was on your side. He was trying to help you. He believed in your cause, sacrificed for it." *As did Alani, whom you also tried to frame,* K.O. added silently.

Ben sat down again and picked up the chisel, toying with it. He ran a thumb along its sharpened edge, caressing the blade.

Donna had stopped crying, so K.O. risked a look. Donna gave her a small nod. She seemed to be back. For how long was the question. God only knew what she had been through the last two days.

Ben cocked his head to look at her. In the silence, the sound of his callused thumb scratching against the steel was like sandpaper. K.O. met his gaze. "I guess it doesn't matter now. Two more *haoles* won't be talking by tomorrow morning."

He said it so matter of factly that it took K.O. a beat to process it. Her brain spun with too few options while he began to speak.

"I joined the HCS when I was twenty. Soon I realized there was an undercurrent of deeper politics if I wanted to take advantage of it . . . which I did. All my life I've lived on or near this homestead; these lands, handed down from generation to generation, protected and revered. Suddenly, some white government was going to take it away from us? Not if I could stop it. *Ka Leo* opened doors for me. They would help me in my fight if I would become a soldier for theirs. It was an easy choice."

He had stopped rubbing the chisel and had begun flipping it, end over end, catching it with incredible ease. K.O. was fascinated that he didn't need to watch it to catch it. She made herself pay attention to the words.

"I became more useful to them, more knowledgeable in the way the organizations worked in tandem for a similar goal, but in such different ways. We recruited new soldiers, trained them, sent them out to get jobs in helpful industries like I did in this job."

K.O.'s mind flitted to the question of how many jobs, agencies, might be affected by this "double-agent" project.

Scary. What was going to happen? If he was accurate—and she didn't have any reason to doubt him in this arena, given the rallies, riots, vandalism, and rising violence—was there some nuclear meltdown equivalent in the political realm looming on the horizon?

"So what were you supposed to do?"

"We educated people about our history and cause. Our numbers swelled as we gained power and recognition."

"Why didn't I ever see you at any rallies or in the press?"

"I was supposed to stay undercover."

"You did a great job. I think I'm beginning to see what

happened to Blala Richards." K.O.'s arms were almost completely
numb. She wiggled her fingers, trying to maintain some circulation,
should she be given an opportunity to use them.

"Do you?"

"Yes. You did as much work as everyone else, but you didn't
get the recognition." She saw his eyes narrow and knew she was
on the right track. "And although that might be nice for a while,
you got tired of it."

"I did *more* than everyone else!" He slammed the chisel on the
table. "I took risks! I killed Ellis for them! For him!"

"Who?" K.O. watched, ready to lunge if he went for her or
Donna.

"Kepa."

"Nahua ordered the hit?"

"No! That was my gift to the cause."

"How was that a gift? It was your land at stake. What did that
do for the group?"

"Ours came first. But others would be next. That is how it
always is with you."

By "you," K.O. assumed he meant whites, but he could have
meant the government. His eyes bulged and he rolled the chisel
between his hands as if to crush it.

"Do you think Ellis would stop at our lands? He wanted more
for his golf course. Do you think one golf course would be enough?
Not when so much money is at stake."

"What did the government have to do with a golf course? I
thought they were negotiating for stewardship. You said the lands
could never be taken."

"They can't. But your courts can tie up our lands, drain our
funds, harm our future, bind our freedom. I don't know what
your government thought Ellis was doing, but I know he was
working a private deal and was clearing title to other land from
back doors, so he could get a piece of the action on the sale. Maybe
your government was hoping for a loophole so you could sell a

lease hold parcel to the highest bidder or add another military outpost. Maybe he was working on his own. I don't know, but I solved the problem for everyone."

K.O. had trouble following his twists and turns of logic. He seemed to be mixing the golf course and Ellis with his grandfather's eviction for back taxes and other land acquisitions.

He was probably right, in any case. Land in Hawai'i was a political minefield and people had died throughout history protecting it and trying to steal it. Not much had changed in five hundred years. More or less.

K.O. remembered bits of one of her conversations with Roly a lifetime ago. Kepa Nahua was being investigated for money laundering in the timeshares deal, and a thread of that had been tied to the golf course consortium and stewardship mess. They had evidence that Kepa was playing both sides. He had been skimming off money not only into *Ka Leo,* but into his own pockets, too. How ironic that Tiny Sugano tried to help his boss in both their noble causes, but misguided ways, when in reality he was helping Nahua against his own family. She decided it would not be prudent to point this out right now. Her hands ached from a lack of circulation and her bladder complained.

"I'm clear on why you killed Ellis." K.O. understood the passion behind the Homelands and his animosity towards those who wanted to use Hawaiian land for yet another of a zillion golf courses. She supposed he had defiled the burial site in order to direct suspicion towards a *haole.* But she felt she was running out of time and that was less important than her next question. "But you killed Blala Richards because he got the recognition you felt you deserved?"

"I did, and do deserve!" he snarled, pausing in his chisel rolling. "But not just that. It was becoming obvious to me that unless I did something, I was never going to move up any higher in *Ka Leo.* Kepa would never see that I was doing all the work, all the dirty work, and I was never going any farther than I am now." He stood and paced in the small kitchen, voice rising passionately. "I should have been at Kepa's side in those rallies. I should have been the one with my picture in the paper!"

Oh, I think you're gonna get your picture in the paper now.

"You killed him so you could be Kepa's 'second-in-command?'"

"That's enough!" His shout echoed through the small house as he stopped and glared at her. "You will never understand, *haole*. Time to go."

He face went vacant. One moment he was ranting—the next, nobody was home.

K.O.'s fear shot so high, it felt as if an electrical charge had gripped the top of her head. The next second her heart dropped into her stomach as he leapt to his feet, slashed the tape holding them both in their chairs, yanked them up, and pushed them towards the back door.

The screen screeched as he used Donna's face to open the door. K.O. added that to her list of crimes for which she would dearly love to have a say in his punishment. If she let him live.

If *she* lived.

CHAPTER THIRTY-SEVEN

The breeze from the nearby bay was chilly as it swept down the valley. K.O. and Donna, arms bound behind them stumbled in the darkness, pushed by the uninhabited body of Ben Kanealiʻihiwi Sugano.

K.O.'s cooling sweat felt icy, and when she accidentally bumped into Donna, she felt just as clammy.

He shoved them up a well-traveled trail farther into the lush valley. K.O. heard rustling sounds from behind her, as if he was removing his clothing, but when she tried to look, he cuffed her again.

"Where are we going?" she asked.

The only response was an animal-like grunt. Her fear mounted. The moon was round and full, and her eyes had quickly adapted to the night. She could see the trail clearly ahead as it wound higher up the valley. On her left, it had risen above the valley floor, and although she could not see the drop because of the heavy undergrowth, she could hear the stream rushing farther away with each turn of the path. In the lead, Donna had the difficult job of navigating over and around every root and rock. Her strain and exhaustion were evident and growing with every step. K.O., in the middle, tried to stay close to her, if only to provide comfort.

She shook her fingers again, attempting to keep the tingling at bay. She noticed she had a little more wiggle room now, and felt the tape carefully, knowing Sugano was directly behind her. She allowed herself a slim hope as she detected a tiny tear. When he had cut them loose from the chairs, he must have nicked the tape binding her wrists.

From behind her, all she heard were his gentle breaths. He moved quietly, with ease on this ancient path, his breathing unstrained, although the trail continued to ascend steeply. K.O. was in good physical shape, but her breath rasped harshly. Donna's sounded even worse, compounded by two days of captivity.

In the dark patches of the trail, where banana *poka* vine choked the bright moon and their captor could not see, K.O. twisted and pulled at her binding. She imagined each fiber of the tape giving way, although she could not be sure that it was. She couldn't bear the idea that it wasn't.

The women needed no prodding now. There was nowhere to go. The trail was one person wide, falling steeply to the icy, rocky waters below on their left. Another cliff rose to their right, so covered in banyan, banana, vines, and shadow, no hope of escape lay that way.

K.O.'s mind raced with possibilities, all borne of desperation, all impossible. She had no purse—no weapons—nothing. She was tired from the strain of their kidnapping and becoming physically exhausted from the long climb. Ben seemed to be able to hike forever. He obviously had a goal. K.O. hoped they would reach it soon. She couldn't imagine how Donna managed to forge ahead, one step after another, in darkness both mental and physical.

Could she turn fast enough to push him off the cliff? He had maintained a safe distance from them since the first push, and the trail had narrowed.

She listened carefully to his breathing. It seemed even fainter. Did she want to risk turning to look and getting hit in the head again? How many blows to the head could she take and still be able to think? Better to wait until she had room, until an opportunity presented itself. He was going to an awful lot of trouble, and she figured he had some sort of fancy death scenario in mind. She was sure he wouldn't kill them simply. Pretty sure.

The trail wound ever up, and she began to hear a rushing sound that filled her with dread. She knew where she was now, and where he was taking them. Yes, the trail would open out soon, but it would not be to her advantage.

Only moments later, they stepped into a large clearing so filled with sound that she could not hear her heartbeat or her own labored breathing. He had brought them to the top of the falls. Water raced over boulders, a wide river of sound that silenced all with its force. K.O. knew these falls. They were in every tourist brochure as the most magnificent in the islands. Ancient, revered, spiritual, ceremonial. Hawaiians still used the site for prayers, rituals, and sacrifice. Modern sacrifice had been changed to fruit, flowers, and alcohol, but the ancient gods demanded blood.

Sixty feet from where she stood to the bottom. K.O. calculated the odds of surviving a fall. Rocks lined the basin, but she had jumped from half-way up into the pool in her early reckless years in the islands. The pool was a hundred feet across and fairly shallow, except for that one deep spot where the locals jumped. If they were pushed, could she hit that spot, in the dark, exhausted, afraid? Could she take Donna with her? She almost laughed hysterically as she wondered if Donna could even swim. What an irony to survive the fall only to drown.

She had to do something, though. This was her window, her one opportunity. Donna had stopped as soon as she had come into the clearing, twenty feet from the edge of the hungry river. K.O. passed her, hoping to communicate somehow with her.

She turned back but said nothing. What she saw startled her into silence.

They were utterly alone. Ben Sugano had disappeared.

CHAPTER THIRTY-EIGHT

Scarcely believing her eyes, K.O. carefully turned and scanned the gloomy jungle. The moon spotlighted the clearing at the apex of the cascade. She and Donna stood in plain view, surrounded by dense undergrowth. Shadows cut the foliage into sharp relief. Donna's face was devoid of color and expression. From the blue-white light or fear, K.O. could not tell.

A breeze, untempered by any barrier down the rushing river, wrapped them in cloaks of ice. Slowly K.O. moved to Donna's side, her eyes continually scanning the dark.

Donna had not moved, but as K.O. approached, she saw that Donna was indeed home and was also searching for Ben. They shivered in their thin T-shirts and huddled for warmth.

"Do you see him?" K.O. barely whispered, although the river obscured any other sound. She did not believe that Sugano had left them entirely alone, or had gone for good. The way she felt now, she could imagine him having super-hearing like the Bionic Woman.

Just perfect. A close-up shot of Lindsey Wagner's ear "listening" popped into K.O.'s head.

Donna shook her head. "Do you have any ideas?"

It was K.O.'s turn to shake hers. "No. But I'm sure he's not through with us, yet." She felt Donna tremble beside her. "We'll come up with something. The key here is not to panic." *Great advice Ogden. Now do something.*

She put her mouth right against Donna's ear, trying to look as if she were just cuddling for warmth. "I think my tape can be torn. I'm sure I felt it give when he cut us loose. Maybe yours did, too. I'm going to turn so we're back to back. See if we can edge out of this damn light." At any other time, the brilliant moonlight would have seemed the epitome of romance, but tonight, it meant danger.

The women kept a wary eye on the boundary of the clearing as they carefully made their way into a sheltered spot. The tension made K.O.'s stomach knot. The continuous stream of adrenalin, the unresolved fight-or-flight response, weakened her, until she felt unable to remain standing. Her good sense told her to stay ready to run, but her body could no longer comply. Again, she marveled at Donna's strength in enduring her two-day ordeal, plus hiking up the mountain in the dark to this sacrificial plateau.

The women sank to the wet, rotting jungle floor, outside the circle of light. They sat back to back and weakly picked at each other's tape. K.O. felt that hers was in fact torn, but Donna was too weak to rip it. She tugged at Donna's restraints. Tears pricked her eyes as she heard Donna groan in pain and felt blood trickling down her hands. The tape refused to give.

K.O. was startled out of a light doze by a crackle of under-growth, as something large moved towards the clearing near them. Ben Sugano was coming back. They hadn't formulated a plan. They were too weak and afraid.

Donna had no reserves left to fight, so it was K.O. against a two hundred pound man who was probably certifiable. She refused to consider leaving Donna and going for help. She was terrified that he would kill Donna in his anger, but she was unable to conceive of a plan to get them off the mountain together safely.

The breeze shook the trees raggedly and the air smelled of rain. Ben appeared at the far edge of the clearing. He had, indeed, removed his western clothing and now wore only a *malo*—a loincloth. K.O. felt the same fear that had gripped her in Blala's presence. Ben Sugano was a mountain of solid muscle. The seemingly flabby, out-of-shape office worker had completely disappeared, and in his place stood a thousand year old warrior.

He stepped into the bright light and saw them instantly, their efforts to burrow into the jungle and safety nothing but a mockery. What K.O. had taken for shadows on his body, thrown from the writhing branches, she now saw were tattoos. A necklace as wide as an Egyptian breastplate spread over his collar bones, disappearing over his shoulders. Wide bands of geometric patterns encircled his upper arms, and calves, and those on his thighs continued up under the *malo*.

He crossed the clearing in huge strides, and when he stood over them, K.O. saw a knife sheathed in his loincloth. He carried a stick—a spear—taller than himself, and whittled to a wicked point. Legs spread, he folded his arms and frowned.

"Ben?" K.O. whispered.

A short, sharp shake of the head. *I guess Ben's not home anymore, either.*

"Get up."

K.O. stood first and carefully helped Donna, who rose stiffly, but unresisting. K.O. hoped that was a good sign, but couldn't be sure.

Ben remained immobile, and as unforgiving as a tree. She had no doubt he intended to finish them off in some gruesome and primitive way. But she also thought that if she caused enough trouble, he'd happily modify his plans and end it instantly.

"Move." He opened his arms, and the spear angled out indicating the edge of the falls.

K.O.'s brain whirled furiously as she picked her way through the rocky shallows to the edge of the falls. With their arms bound, she and Donna stood no chance of protecting themselves if he pushed them over. *That was assuming they were still alive when they did go over,* she thought.

Donna suddenly collapsed in a heap. "I can't move. My ankle, I twisted it." The moonlight showed tears tracking as she sat awkwardly, her ankle jutting over the rock tumble of the shallows.

Ben stopped. K.O. stopped, too, and looked at Ben. His stone face angled towards Donna, and he placed one hand on the knife at his waist.

"I want you to move." His words were said softly, almost without command, but K.O. felt the last bits of his sanity riding on them. She swallowed back the nausea that her fear engendered and bent to help Donna. As she let the other woman lean on her and awkwardly rise, she thought she heard her whisper, "Swim."

Donna swayed unsteadily on her feet, but she caught K.O.'s eye. K.O. felt strength in that gaze and trusted her friend. Donna swayed again and leaned on her for balance. K.O. felt her shove something into her bound hands before she pushed off again saying, "I'm okay. Just dizzy."

Both women faced Ben, their backs to the roaring water. K.O. had thought her fear could not be any greater, but she had been mistaken. She knew Donna had seen the same thing she had seen, for her body had gone as rigid as a post.

Ben managed one step towards the women, a smirk of triumph on his face at the sight of their abject terror and submission, before he realized their fear was not for him. He turned slowly and froze.

A giant feral pig stood only yards away in the clearing. Tusks gleamed in the light, and dark bristles covered the muscular body as it raised its snout and sniffed, taking another step closer. As it assessed its quarry, K.O. saw the pendulous teats of a nursing mother and realized they were *all* dead. Somewhere near this clearing was the reason for the pig's concern. Ben's insane scheme to claim an esteemed position in Hawaiian culture was about to be derailed by piglets.

The irony did not escape her; however, the mother seemed quite serious about thoroughly removing the interlopers.

Another gruesome thought occurred to K.O. Pigs would eat a dead body.

Bodies, she amended. *Yuck.*

She felt a poke in her back from Donna who had moved closer to the edge of the falls even as the pig moved nearer to them.

Ben stood his ground, apparently unsure how this twist fit into his plans, but not reacting to the danger K.O. knew was there.

He was too far from cover. No tree, rock, or other protection was within reach before a racing, enraged mother could gore him. He had chosen his spot for his victims well, but now it appeared it might be his downfall, and their saving grace. K.O. thought he must feel extremely vulnerable in only a loincloth, but couldn't bring herself to care.

She received another poke from Donna. When she turned to look, Donna nodded at the thing she had put into K.O.'s hands, but that K.O. had completely forgotten.

It was a rock. A little pointy—not a great rock, but a rock nonetheless. As K.O. wondered how she could throw it from behind her at Ben with enough force to do any damage, Donna moved her arms slightly apart and K.O.'s jaw dropped. *Duh.* Donna was showing her that she had cut her tape with a rock and her hands were free.

Thank God someone is using her brain, K.O. chided herself. *What the hell did I go to school for, anyway?*

She sawed at her tape, while watching the surreal spectacle in the clearing. The pig had closed the distance between itself and Ben. Then a number of things happened at once.

Ben threw his spear, just as the pig charged. The rock was working its way through K.O.'s tape, and the two women were making their way towards the jungle and safety, when the pig hit Ben. His piercing scream as the pig's tusks ripped into him was terrifying. The women had not moved far enough away from the edge. The force of several hundred pounds of impaled pig, added to a large man, crashed into them. The rushing water and slippery rocks added to their momentum and sent them over the edge into a fall of sixty feet of icy, rocky, rushing water.

CHAPTER THIRTY-NINE

As K.O. sailed over the edge, the seconds before she hit the water were filled with machine-gun thoughts: *Don't hit the rocks. Keep away from the pig. And Ben. And Donna. Any of them hitting me could mean death. I lost my rock.*

When she hit the water, her first inclination was to bounce back up for air, but she denied herself that pleasure and dove even deeper, hoping to avoid a pile-up with herself as the airbag.

In the spill of the falls, she sensed, more than heard, the crash of the others as they plummeted around her. The shock of cold water pushed the air from her lungs, and she struggled away from the noise to where she thought shallower water lay.

She found the boulders lining the edge surprisingly warm as she hugged them, resting her cheek and letting her body float, before she could pull herself out of the water enough to look around.

With some surprise she saw that her hands had indeed been freed, but each wrist was still encircled with a silver duct tape bracelet. She somehow expected the roaring to lessen since she was resting, but the sound pounded on and pressed against her head like a helmet of noise. She used her raw hands to pull herself towards the falls and turn to search for Donna.

The moon lit the pool. K.O. scanned it quickly, seeing no one. Her heart lurched as she forced herself to look more slowly and thoroughly. She knew that powerful falls often trapped things directly under them for a time, and she ached to think of Donna pinned underwater for who knew how long while she had pulled herself away and rested.

She warily checked for Ben Sugano but didn't see him. She dreaded searching the pool for her friend. Her hands truly throbbed now and felt as if all the skin had worn off her palms.

A shove came from behind. She whirled, heart racing, arms thrown up in defense. The bristly body of the pig, still with the spear lodged in it, bobbed gently in the eddy.

"Shit! I can't take much more of this." K.O. leaned weakly against the rocks as yet another dose of adrenalin ebbed from her system, leaching her remaining energy.

She forced herself to move, rock by rock, towards the falls, feeling with her feet and one hand at a time for Donna. She was able to pull herself behind the cataract to a small ledge and rest for a moment, but guilt and desperation pressed her to continue.

She circled the pool and had arrived at a small beach where intrepid hikers could easily step into the frigid waters, when her strength gave out entirely.

"I'll just lie here for a minute. Then I'll start diving." As she lay there, it occurred to her that she had probably hit her head on something or someone on the way down. That could be the only explanation for not worrying about Sugano, right?

She woke up with a start. The pool was dark; the moon had set. Her legs, still in the water, were numb. As she cradled her head, she smelled blood on her hands. Nothing on her body felt as if it was hers, but everything hurt. She remembered in a flash where she was and why. The thought of diving into the black lagoon to recover Donna's body brought a gush of noisy tears. She painfully rolled herself over from her front to her back. A stab of panic coursed through her as a hand, cold and clammy as clay, touched her face.

She screamed and tried to roll away, but lacked the strength.

"Sssshhh."

"Donna?" Half query, half prayer.

The hand flitted like a cobweb to K.O.'s shoulder and patted her.

Fresh tears fell as K.O. reached out and took Donna's hand in her own. "Are you okay?"

"Yes." A sigh.

"We have to get out of here."

No answer.

"Donna!" K.O. rolled onto her side and gripped Donna's slack hand. "Come on. We have to go."

Pre-dawn light, cold and gray, filtered through the top of the jungle. It had rained, and K.O. was covered in a fine mud from the beach.

She pushed herself to her knees and crawled to Donna who lay on her back. Her pale skin was waxy, and her hair had dried into long ropes. If not for the trickle of blood on her face, K.O. thought she would have looked like a surreal mermaid caught in a half-spell. She gently shook her friend.

Donna opened her eyes and nodded when K.O. held her gaze. K.O. pulled her to a wobbly sitting position and they both breathed heavily, resting.

"Sorry," Donna said. "I haven't eaten for two days . . . . Three days."

K.O.'s mind flew to her pocket. She dragged out three wet, wrapped peppermints and thrust them into Donna's hand. "Wait, wait." She took them back and laboriously unwrapped them, struggling with the wet plastic, trying to remember how long they'd been in her pocket. Then she pushed one into Donna's mouth.

Donna's eyes opened wider as the spicy mint hit her taste buds. K.O. watched as she worked the candy around her mouth until she quickly chewed it and swallowed. K.O. gave her the remaining candies.

"Come on, girl. Gotta go." K.O. slung Donna's arm over her shoulder then wrapped her own arm around Donna's waist and lifted.

"Jeez, what have you been eating, girl?" she said as they swayed upright.

A snort from Donna was her reward. She struggled to keep her footing on the muddy, pebbled shore and made her way up the bank to the lower path she knew was there.

"Where's Tiny?" Donna mumbled when they reached the path and had stopped again.

"Dunno. Gotta keep moving." K.O. had no idea where to move to. That was the problem. She felt exposed here, but knew it was miles to the homestead, assuming she could even get them there.

She couldn't hope for Kumu Kaneali'ihiwi to be home and help them. She didn't know if Ben was dead. Best not to count on that. They could wait for days or weeks for a wayward hiker to this revered but remote location.

The homestead was the only place around. Her car was there; a phone was there. Possibly, Ben was there. *Shit.* No choice.

She hitched Donna's arm higher on her shoulders and started walking and talking. Saying anything to keep her feet moving, and to hear Donna's labored breathing.

Her mind drifted to a childhood, Christmas-cartoon song about the abominable snowman or some such creature, exhorting hope.

She sang for both of them, in time with her wheezing. "Put one foot in front of the other. Soon you'll be walkin' cross the floooooor. Put one foot in front of the other. And soon you'll be walkin' out the door."

CHAPTER FORTY

Icy drops fell down the neck of K.O.'s ragged T-shirt, trickling down her spine and sending violent shivers that threatened to tip her and Donna over. The jungle was slowly warming and lightening with the coming dawn, but not fast enough for K.O.

It seemed they had to stop and rest every few steps, although K.O. told herself they were doing fine, that it only seemed that way. This lower path followed the stream and was less steep and more comfortable to walk on. *Comfort being a relative term,* she thought morosely.

Heliconia and ginger towered over them, shading an already cool trail. Birds woke, and their noisy rustling and squabbling as they started their day reassured K.O. that all was well in the brush. At least, nothing human lurked there, since as the women shuffled past, the birdsong stopped abruptly, followed by a flurry of birds on the wing, and then a cacophonous bout of avian scolding.

As the day brightened, K.O. discovered that both she and Donna were covered in dirt, dried blood—not in life-threatening amounts—and smears of unknown sources. Donna had lost her shoes, K.O. assumed in the water, and now limped painfully along. K.O. would have gladly given her shoes to Donna, but knew from previous mutual shoe coveting, they would not fit.

During one of their earlier meetings in court on a case, they had both exclaimed simultaneously, "I like your shoes!" Then both had laughed and said, "Penthouse," referring to Liberty House department store's discount shop. K.O. frequented the downtown location whenever she had a court case, and as it turned out, so did Donna.

To their disappointment, however, their shoes were a full size apart, thereby effectively terminating any hope of shoe trades. But on a happier note, they wore the same size in clothing. Dresses, tops, and mini-skirts had flown across the island, and occasional wardrobe emergency calls had been treated as seriously as medical interventions. They knew each other's closets intimately, and often would buy something for the other, the payoff being that if the receiver didn't want it, the giver would.

K.O. smiled as her thoughts flitted over the memories. She silently promised Donna a new pair of shoes from the Penthouse after this.

Donna sagged, and K.O. gently set her down. Neither had energy for conversation anymore. No more songs or stories. Initially, K.O. had kept her attention on the surrounding jungle, looking for any sign of ambush from Sugano. Or even feral pigs.

As the morning passed, however, and her strength had ebbed, she had concentrated more on just getting to the homestead. As she replayed the tumble over the falls again in her mind, she doubted Ben could have survived a goring and a sixty foot header. In the seconds before she had gone over, blood had spouted from him, and his scream alone had indicated a severe injury. She and Donna had both hit the deeper, but narrow central part of the pool under the falls. Had there been room for a third person?

Maybe—if, as she had thought, she had hit first, then Donna, then Ben who was farthest from the edge. Then, perhaps, they all had survived the bowl of rocks.

He must have bled a lot, though. She could not be sure where the pig had hit him, but it appeared to have launched itself pretty well. Either in the abdomen—probably fatal—or the groin— definitely painful, and with that nice, big femoral artery to rip. Either way, not great odds for survival. As these happy thoughts occurred, they rejuvenated K.O. enough to heft Donna up once again. And, as she stepped onward, the trail opened up and she recognized the widening and browning of the river, which signified its proximity to the sea, which meant, they were nearing the homestead. Finally.

She eased Donna down in a sheltered spot, protected from passersby.

"I'm going on ahead to make sure it's safe. Stay here. I'll come back for you."

Donna shook her head.

"Yes, I have to. You're too weak, and if it comes to a fight, I can't worry about you."

Donna sighed and nodded, her eyes never leaving K.O.'s. "What are you going to do?"

"I'm going to get my gun first, then my keys. And drive us the hell out of here."

"Call 911?"

"Not from here I'm not. We're getting out. We'll call from the hospital. I'm taking you there first."

K.O. thought Donna would protest, but she only nodded. "Okay."

"Stay here. I really don't think he could have survived that pig and the fall, but you never know. I'll be back."

K.O. didn't look back because she didn't want to see any doubt on Donna's face. She felt like an Indian in a spaghetti western, sneaking up on the fort. Her clothing, dried now to a crackly crunch, snapped with every step. *At least I blend into the scenery,* she figured, as she circled the house from the rear.

The dwelling looked the same as when she'd last seen it. *When was it? Yesterday?* A year ago? She wasn't sure, and that scared her as much as actually going up to the house.

She checked the garage. The unknown car was still there. She assumed it was the *kumu's,* but if so, and he was away as Ben had claimed, why wouldn't he have taken it? It wasn't like a neighbor could just pop over and drive him to the airport like a normal thing. Maybe it was Sugano's instead.

The gleam of metal caught her eye, and she entered the rickety building, skirting the vehicle. A small workbench stretched across the back of the structure—ancient, devoid of much except desiccated bug bodies. She did see a broken tool rack hanging askew above the table. The gleam she had noticed was from the blade of a shattered chisel caught in the rack.

K.O. pocketed it, at the same time feeling a smooth, round shape. She pulled out another mint and gratefully unwrapped it. The tang and the sugar made her feel better instantly. She checked the rest of the building for anything else that might come in handy. The car was locked and didn't appear to hold anything worth breaking in for. Discarded rubbish, an old shoe, a piece of tarp, nothing much.

It was time to head for the house. She peeked through a crack at the garage door and watched the main house for a few moments. Her stomach growled with the tease of the mint, and she absently hushed it. She felt only a little nervous, and was heartened by the thought that if Ben was in there, she was probably physically the stronger now. She hoped.

She felt almost naked as she crossed the yard from the garage to the house. The back door was closed. Had Ben left it open when they'd started this nightmare? She couldn't remember. Only last night.

"Jesus." *Don't go there. Don't go there,* she admonished herself. Unbidden, flashes of the last few days raced across her vision. Donna's face, forcing open that same screen door. The chisel, rocking back and forth on the kitchen table, the sound of it unnaturally loud in the fear-filled silence. Donna's wrists, bleeding onto the floor while she stared vacantly. Ben in Donna's office, calmly discussing crime scenes that he had created.

K.O. started. She realized she'd been standing, unmoving and exposed on the back porch for too long. The yard was empty, the house felt empty, but who really knew?

She opened the screen door. The screech was audible for a thousand miles. Sweat popped out in a flood, drenching her. She wiped her forehead with her filthy tee and tried the handle to the inner door. It turned easily and swung open. The screen closed with another screech.

"Great. Just great." Better than an alarm. She stood just inside the door and surveyed the kitchen. The roll of duct tape still where he had left it. Chisel gone.

Had he taken it with him last night or put it somewhere? God, she couldn't think.

He had thrown her purse on the kitchen counter, hadn't he? It wasn't there now. It had her gun in it. She had another in her car, but the keys were in her purse, too. If he had her gun, or even his original weapon, and was waiting for her in the house, she was toast.

She swallowed a huge lump and moved cement feet slowly around the edge of the kitchen, by the counters, cabinets, looking, opening doors, for her purse. Keys. Gun. No luck.

"Shit," she whispered. She even opened the refrigerator and freezer. Nothing. The hallway to the living-room was dark, and the rooms beyond, darker still. She would be lit as a perfect target the moment she stepped from kitchen to hall. Well . . . nothing for it now.

She stepped, and almost had a heart attack as the refrigerator motor kicked on with a thump and a roar. She flattened herself against the wall and dropped, scuttling to the living-room, past closed doors, to bedrooms, she assumed.

If I'd had any liquid in me at all, I'd have wet my pants, she thought as she hid behind an overstuffed chair with a high back.

She waited for her heart to resume a normal rate. Her gasping slowed to merely panicked panting, and she spied her purse on the coffee table, sitting two feet in front of her hiding place.

Carefully scanning the room, she eased from behind her dubious cover and snatched her purse from the table. It felt heavy and she sighed, hoping it contained her weapon.

She crawled back to her chair and hitched the bag into her lap. In the semi-gloom she carefully poured the contents out. *Keys, thank God.* Her initial glance told her the gun was gone, and her heart sank. A thousand receipts, business cards, and scraps of paper. An extremely old Snickers bar.

She ate it in two bites, savoring the headrush from the sugar, her teeth aching from chewing something. *Jeez, it's only been a day. Well, a day and a half. Of hell.* Lipstick, hairbrush, wallet—nothing else missing. A couple Flex-cuffs.

She put her head in her hands, finally accepting what she had pushed so far away. The gun was gone, and she was on her own.

At least she had her keys. She could get Donna and drive them both to safety. Maybe she could call 911 from here.

Good sense and experience told her that Ben had not survived such injuries, but her own history of luck told her he had, and that he was so bent upon revenge and his own plot that stubbornness would have taken him back here—to where he knew the women would have to come in order to save themselves.

The phone resolved one issue by its absence. The living-room had no phone that she could see. That left the phone on the wall in the kitchen. Passing the closed bedroom doors through the funnel of light was not something she felt was wise, but she saw no other choice. If she could call for help, then get Donna to the car, they could make it out. Just maybe.

Call it cowardice, but I am not opening those bedroom doors for all the Tequila Shooters in China, she thought. *If he ain't come to get me yet, I ain't lookin'.*

She quickly passed down the hall to the kitchen. *Is that door just a bit open, now? No, it's not,* she insisted.

She picked up the receiver and leaned, back against the wall, to dial. Several long seconds passed before she realized she had no dial tone.

That moment galvanized her into action and she flew out the back door, purse slung around her body, keys in her pocket, heedless of noise, and ran for the jungle and Donna.

CHAPTER FORTY-ONE

K.O. had to slow to a trot, then a limping walk. She had left Donna farther from the homestead than she'd thought. The sun was high and hot as she returned to caution. The path became familiar, and she had so completely prepared herself for Ben either to have taken Donna again, or harmed her, that she cried in relief when she saw Donna's curled form in the nest of jungle.

K.O. crashed to a halt and shook her friend rather more roughly than was needed. Donna's eyes flew open, registering alarm.

"Sorry, sorry. It's okay." K.O. hugged her. "I was just worried. I have the car keys. Let's go." She struggled to help Donna to her feet, guilty for a moment for eating the whole Snickers herself. "I'll buy you a huge dinner tomorrow."

Donna looked puzzled, but nodded. K.O. dragged her towards the homestead.

"Where is he?" Donna whispered.

"I don't know. I didn't see him." K.O. decided not to mention the gun—guns—or lack thereof.

She kept a wary eye out as they approached the garage, but nothing had changed. The distant sound of surf was soothing. The landscape gently waved in an unseen breeze that brought the heady smell of plumeria from the trees in the front yard. K.O. held her breath, watched the covered windows, and prayed, as they rounded the corner of the house to where she had parked. She could see the car, safe and snug, a sanctuary. Her gaze flicked back and forth across the property, waiting for a figure to launch from the house or the garage.

Her heartbeat was audible above the distant surf. As she approached the passenger side of the car, she held the keys in her hand. She gently leaned Donna against the back door, warm and comforting from the morning sun.

Donna closed her eyes while K.O. fumbled with the lock and finally heard the click of the release.

She was turning to help Donna, when Donna screamed long and loud, and collapsed—seeming to be sucked down, rather than falling. Watching in horror, K.O. lost precious seconds. Then she grabbed Donna's arms, even as a bloody set of hands pulled against her from under the vehicle.

Donna's leg was slashed and bleeding profusely. It hindered Ben's efforts to drag her down. She could no longer stand, so K.O. had to support her and pull at the same time. She was desperate to keep Donna from disappearing under the Crown Vic.

Donna got her one good leg underneath her and shoved. Combined with K.O.'s terror-boosted strength, this managed to pull Ben partially from his site of ambush.

He didn't look human. His face—contorted with rage—was caked with blood. A flap of skin from his skull—probably torn during his fall at the pool—hung macabrely over one ear. Burst blood vessels in his eyes and dilated pupils added to the horror of his look.

"Jesus Christ!" K.O. shouted as she fought. Thank God Donna couldn't see him clearly.

Then, Ben changed his plan. He let go and sent the women reeling from the safety of the car. He scrambled out from under it, chisel still in his hand, and they received the full impact of his wounds and his insanity. The pig had gored him in the groin. The tusks had missed the femoral artery, but enough blood had flowed to coat his legs and weaken him.

But not enough. His loin cloth was filthy, stiff, and drenched with blood, gore and dirt. K.O. marveled that the fall into clean water had not even helped his appearance.

He looked immense. His muscles were rigid and swollen— from fear, pain, or mental collapse, K.O. couldn't tell.

In the seconds it took her to make this assessment, Ben staggered forward, leading with his chisel. K.O. gained her feet and pushed Donna towards a palm tree, never taking her eyes off the chisel. She heard Donna's scooting and hoped she had reached the relative protection of its sturdy trunk.

"Hey, asshole!" K.O. waved at Ben and stepped towards the front of her car. Her other gun was inside the glove compartment, but he was blocking the passenger door. She wanted him to follow her to the driver's side, to put the car between him and Donna.

Ben shook his head like an angry bull.

"Yeah, that's it ya big *moke*. You wanted a *haole* sacrifice, now you got one." K.O. waited until he was focused on her before she took another step. He swung his weapon in a weak arc, but it still made her nervous. What if he was faking his weakness? What if he could lunge and stab, leaving her skewered and Donna unprotected.

She took a deep breath and feined a leg cramp. Not much of a trick, given the state of her body.

"Why'd you do it, Tiny?" She deliberately used the nickname he seemed to hate. She stepped around the front of the car.

"Kaneali'ihiwi!" he shouted and swung the chisel again. The click and scrape of the chisel on the hood sounded like a blade on bone.

The breeze blew the plumeria, still thick with fragrance. *Something should be different if we're going to die.*

"I am my people." He took another step, and K.O. was at the driver's door.

"Your people think you're crazy. Who's out here with you, huh? Any of your people?" Her tone was deliberately derisive, taunting, and she watched his eyes narrow, the pupils contract in anger.

How does he do that? But she'd spent enough time with animals to read them and understand when the stand off was over. It was over.

Just as he jumped for her, she wondered if she'd turned the key in the lock the right way—the way that unlocked all the doors, not just that one.

You are an idiot, she chastised herself,but found that the door was indeed unlocked. As she pulled, she tripped backwards, however, and only the opening of the door saved her from a vicious stab. She held onto the handle as she fell and felt the vibration of the blade as it screeched down the glass . Her legs flew under the opening door, and she tucked them turtle-like, as the chisel continued down the outside of the door.

Ben let out a primal yell and fought her for the door. She scuttled through it into the front seat. She knew she could not wrestle the door shut in time, so she dove for the glove box, awkwardly stretching across the automatic gear shift and all her junk in the passenger seat.

She opened the compartment and blindly grabbed for the familiar shape and weight. Instinctively she kicked and caught a part of him—a howl and the graze of the blade down the outside of her jeans leg told her.

She felt her .38 and rolled back, crammed at an angle against the far door and seatbacks, aiming for the open door.

"Stop, stop, stop! Jesus, stop!" Her kick had deflected Ben in his weakened, unbalanced state. But he picked himself up and leaned in the doorjamb, thrusting with his chisel. She curled up her legs and aimed through them screaming, "Stop!" one more time.

He didn't stop.

She fired.

CHAPTER FORTY-TWO

In the ensuing silence, K.O. remained frozen, her hands clenched around the .38, arms rigid, knees bent.

Her neck suddenly screamed, bent as it was against the passenger door, the door handle nearly implanted in her head.

When Ben had fallen out of the car, he had landed with a solid thud and hadn't moved or made a sound. The last thing K.O. wanted to do was go towards him, but it was safer than leaving through the passenger door and walking around the vehicle, when she would have him out of her sight for even those few seconds.

She swallowed hard and shifted her body, to sit up slowly and relieve the pressure on her neck. Then she lowered her weapon and scooted her legs out the driver's door. The door was open wide. The shot had pushed Ben back from the opening. His lower body lay stretched at an angle directly in front of her, but she couldn't see his face. She could see, however, that her shot had taken him low in the abdomen, just inches above the pig's damage.

She could also see the rise and fall of his battered chest.

She stood to get a good look at his face. His eyes were closed at last and he seemed to be resting, arms outflung. The odd patch of torn skin had flipped back into place, and she studied it absently. Unconcious, he looked again like Tiny, the guy from the M.E.'s office.

She searched for the crazy warrior but didn't see him. She hoped that persona wasn't lurking somewhere under the closed lids.

She felt a little odd putting the Flex-cuffs on him, but would rather have to explain them than be unable to explain because he'd gotten them both.

She stood looking down at him and heard a soft, "Hey," from behind her. Donna was leaning on the hood of the car. K.O. went to her and they hugged. Then she helped Donna into the passenger seat as she'd tried to do so long ago.

The cut on Donna's calf had already stopped bleeding, but K.O. still thought it needed stitches.

She came around the car, sat in the driver's seat, and flicked on her police radio. She called in an emergency and asked for an ambulance and some support.

They waited there in the car, doors open, listening to radio traffic, until sirens overtook the squelch of calls.

A blur of time and K.O. was released from the hospital, but Donna was not. Ben Sugano had been arrested and was being held in the prison ward of the hospital. He was immensely strong, and bets were that he would be out before Donna, but that he would go to the mental hospital for evaluation of fitness to stand trial.

K.O. felt sure he would never take the stand.

After a brief investigation into the discharge of her weapon, she returned to work the following week.

The morning paper revealed that all charges against Alani had been dropped. Ben "Tiny" Kaneali'ihiwi Sugano had been charged with two counts of murder: Larry Ellis and Blala Richards. Kepa Nahua, arrested for timeshare schemes, racketeering and fraud, and a number of other offenses, had nothing to say publicly, but he issued a statement, thinly disguised through the Hawaiian Cultural Society, claiming that Ben Sugano had acted alone. With no one sanctioning his actions, it should not reflect poorly upon the good works of the HCS or its mission as Hawai'i's ambassador to the world. An underground rumbling from *Ka Leo* agreed that Sugano was a nutcase and had nothing to do with them, and the case in no way altered their mission to emancipate Hawaiians.

"Right, right. Rats from a sinking ship," K.O. grumbled to Teresa in their favorite recliner facing the Ko'olau mountains. "You play big, you get hurt big." She stroked the big tabby, and Teresa rolled on her back with pleasure.

Another article outlined the Kaneali'ihiwi homestead issue, and as *kumu* had told her, official documents revealed that the land could never be removed from them or their designees for Hawaiian use and preservation. The issue of taxes was resolved, for further investigation showed certain parcels bequeathed by the royal line, including the Kaneali'ihiwi's, to be exempt.

"All for nothing." K.O. sighed, as she put down the paper. "So much pain, for nothing."

She wasn't even really talking about the homestead issue or sovereignty. Her mind had evaded her core concern, and she had put off confronting it for the weeks this had all taken to shake out.

Alani. She didn't want to see him or talk to him, but felt she must.

She put one hand on Teresa's purring body for strength, and punched in the familiar number. She knew he'd gotten his tools back and had returned home. Knowing him as well as she did, she figured he'd have jumped right back into his life and routine.

"Hello?"

"It's me."

"Hi." An awkward silence. In those few words, she couldn't read anything in his voice.

"Are you working?"

"Yes. I have a lot of orders."

He wasn't going to make this easy.

"I just wanted to call and see how you were." A blatant lie. She wanted him to say come over, I miss you. She wanted another chance. Didn't she?

"I'm working. I have my projects. Life goes on."

His projects. Sovereignty among them. That sure wasn't going to go away anytime soon. He sounded sad. Disappointed maybe. Perhaps she was projecting into his voice what she felt.

"I also wanted to say again that I'm sorry. For causing all those problems for you."

"I know. I believe that now. I didn't for a long time."

K.O. was surprised that he hadn't believed her. She had been filled with equal parts anger at his actions and remorse at hers, and it never occurred to her that he might not have accepted that.

"I'm sorry, too," he continued. "I'm sorry I didn't see Kepa for what he was. Is. I'm sorry you got involved."

She wondered if he meant sticking her nose in where it didn't belong.

"I'm sorry—" he hesitated, "you got hurt. That I hurt you."

"I—" K.O. began—

Just as he said, "We—"

"Go ahead," said K.O.

Alani sighed. She pictured him in his studio garage, large hands cradling the phone, hard body slicked with sweat and sawdust as he worked beautiful wood. Under other circumstances, the sigh could have been romantic, or sexy.

It's amazing, K.O. mused, distracted, that the same sounds have totally different meanings under different circumstances. This sigh made her sad. It was a sigh of letting go. She felt it miles away, over a bunch of inanimate wires, a pulling, pushing, distancing. He was not there for her anymore. He was gone. Maybe temporarily while the dust settled, but maybe not. Her pride would not let her ask.

The need to see him, hold him in her arms, smell his sweat

and skin, touch his wavy, but oh, so soft hair was a physical ache
that she now forced far back into her cells.

"I have to go now," Alani said at last.

Gripping the receiver tightly so it wouldn't shake, K.O. said,
"Okay. Me, too. Take care."

"Yeah. You, too." He hung up, a click so gentle she felt more
than heard it.

K.O. sat with the phone in her hand, willing herself not to
cry.

It didn't work. The first fat tears hit Teresa, and she sat up
indignantly. K.O. softly replaced the receiver in its cradle. Teresa
looked at her mistress carefully and then resettled, her fur quickly
dampening under the onslaught.

K.O. cried until she felt empty. How could something feel so
right and be so wrong? *If we were meant to be together, this will
work out.*

She blinked out at the ribbon falls, sparkles of silver down the
green cliffs, mirroring her own cheeks.

It's not going to work out, she thought. That knowlege made
her head ache even more.

Rain, soft and fresh, hit her lanai and swelled the slim ribbons
to wide cascades. *Love hurts like hell,* she thought. *And I really
didn't even get to experience it.* If she'd told him sooner, maybe it
would have been different.

*If you weren't such a hard-assed chicken, maybe you'd have had
love to fall back on right now. Hard-assed chicken?* She had to laugh
at her description.

"Ah, Christ, Teresa. What an idiot I am. Okay, note to self.
And you're my witness. The next time I fall in love—assuming
there is a next time—no beating around the bush. Tell him. Let it
all hang out. Right?"

Teresa opened her green eyes sagely.

"Right."

CHAPTER FORTY-THREE

K.O. had absolutely no energy left for her next call, so she put it off. As usual. Richard and Abby, back in Seattle, had been much on her mind, but would have to wait. As much as she cared for them, they sucked the life out of her, and she had to steel herself before making such a call. Besides, she had the perfect excuse.

Frying pan to fire, she thought as she held the memo announcing the Sergeant's Exam. Friday. Tomorrow. She'd been carrying the memo around for a week as she continued her test preparations.

She felt ready. Sort of. She'd grilled all her friends, had them grill her. She felt she'd pass the test, but that was not her goal. Her goal was a Sergeant's assignment as well. Only a few openings, and she wanted one. Didn't want to wait for the next openings after all this headache.

She sighed and gathered her notes once more, promising to call Richard and Abby after the test. Long after.

She also promised herself a vacation. *Not time off due to an internal investigation, or hospital time, or sick time, dammit.* A real vacation, if only for a few days. *If I pass this thing—when,* she corrected, *I am going somewhere I've never been.*

Although she'd lived in the islands fifteen years, she had yet to visit them all. The trip to the Big Island had been rather more exciting than she had anticipated, so she thought she'd wait a while before returning. *Hmmm.* Lanai? The Pineapple Isle. Molokai? She'd heard wonderful things about the stone formations there. She also was eager to see the leper settlement, Kalaupapa, Father Damien's life work. A local director she'd done a community-theatre play with once had got the role of Father Damien in a movie. That might be the ticket. So to speak.

Well, she had plenty of time to think about it.

One call she did want to make was to Donna Costello.

"Medical Examiner."

"Hey, seestah. Howzit?" K.O. affected a thick pidgin accent.

"Good, seestah. You?" Donna responded.

"How's work? You holding up okay?"

"Sure. You know me. I'm happiest when I'm ass deep in bodies. Well, you know I prefer really old bodies, like skeletons, but a girl's gotta do what a girl's gotta do."

K.O. laughed. "Yeah, I know. So, you sleeping all right?"

"Most nights." K.O. pictured Donna settling back in her office chair, surrounded by stacks of files chin high. "We haven't really talked since I got out of the hospital, but I wanted to thank you for everything."

K.O. never knew how to respond to thanks in cases, from victims. *Wow.* Donna was a victim. And, she supposed, so was she. Tough line of work, this. So she simply said, "You're welcome. Dinner next week? I did promise to buy you a dinner."

"When did you say that?"

"When you were sort of unconcious. You must have heard me though, because here you are."

Donna laughed and it sounded lovely. "John Dominus." Donna named one of the most expensive restaurants in Honolulu.

"Ho, girl, I'm only a cop. Think I'm made of money?"

"Yeah, well, you better get back on the take or you can't afford me."

"You got that right." The women chatted a bit more and made plans to meet the following week. When K.O. got off the phone she felt as if her world was settling back into its normal cradle.

* * *

Test day was absolutely gorgeous. Crisp white clouds like cotton sat demurely atop the Koʻolau mountains. Traffic was light over the Pali Highway into town. She had found all her test materials, her favorite pens and pencils, everything she even suspected might come in handy. She even wore her lucky socks. Regulation black, but with small red and white koi fish embroidered high on the calf. No one would see them, but she would know.

She parked and entered the building, feeling calm and collected. Prepared even. Something must be wrong.

Materials passed out. Directions given. Time started. K.O. began.

When time was called at the end of the session, K.O. felt confident in her ability to answer all that was put forth.

By the time she had used the restroom and reached her car, she could not have told what had been on the test if her niece and nephew were being held hostage.

"I need a drink." And she knew exactly where she would find what she needed.

Twenty minutes later, she rang George's doorbell. The front door opened.

"Well, just like a bad penny." He smiled and pulled the door wider.

"Don't you have a real job? Do you even work anymore? It's only," K.O. glanced at her watch. "Oh, six o'clock. Jeez that was a long one."

George raised his eyebrows as she marched past him and flopped on the couch, throwing her purse on the coffee table.

"Dare I ask, long what?" George asked with just enough lasciviousness as he followed her and sat in his favorite chair.

"You are a baaad man." K.O. shook her finger at him.

"That's what you love about me. You can't help yourself."

"I know."

"Drink?"

"Absolutely."

And, as usual, they slipped into easy conversation. She caught him up on her perspective of the case that wasn't hers, right up until she had postponed calling Richard and Abby.

"I might have some good news on that," George said.

"We could use some." K.O. curled her feet under her on the couch and pulled a hand-knitted afghan over her lap.

"As in all good legal snarls, we look for the loopholes. I think I've found one that let's your friends off the hook. The building in which the timeshare presentations were held did not belong to the company. They just rented it out. Why they didn't use their own is beyond me, but be that as it may, it helps us now. That corporation had an insurance rider that covers this sort of thing. They didn't mean it to, but it does." He chuckled and chose that moment to refresh his drink. He rose and went into the kitchen. K.O. heard cupboards opening and the refrigerator closing. She leapt off her perch and followed.

"You can't leave it like that! What happened? What do we do?" The afghan trailed behind her like a train.

"I'm hungry. You?"

"I could just slap you!"

"I know. Sit. Okay, I'll spill." K.O. sat. He smiled and set a dish of radishes and carrots on the table.

"I found that the insurance rider covers limited damages to its patrons in the event of criminal activity. Now I know all the hotels and things say they are not liable, but they are. I already had a little chat with them, and since Richard and Abby only put a modest down payment on the timeshare, they were more than happy to come to a quick settlement. I did happen to mention that I would not spread the word about this particular loophole to the thousands of others the timeshare folks have probably bilked, thereby holding this hotel accountable." George positively smirked. "I'm sure lawyers who actually practice this sort of thing will already be on it, but that's not my problem."

He left the kitchen, leaving a stunned, open-mouthed K.O. sitting at the table, half-eaten radish in her hand, wearing the security-blanket like a cape.

She was still like that when he returned moments later, setting with a flourish, a business sized envelope on the place mat in front of her. The addressee was George at his office. The return address was the hotel where Richard and Abby had stayed, and also had their first run-in with Kepa Nahua and Waikiki Tradewinds timeshares.

"Leave that open—you'll catch flies. Then your face will freeze that way." He gently reached over the table and shoved the radish in her mouth. His smile was broad and crinkled up his entire face.

K.O. looked up at him, tears welling. "I can't believe this," she mumbled.

"Just look."

She opened the slit envelope and found a check made out to Richard and Abby for twenty-five thousand dollars. "So much? I thought they only left a deposit?"

"Mental anguish."

"Oh, my God!" She jumped out of her chair and ran to hug him. His laugh was deep and rich.

"It's not often I can catch you out, Scarlet," he said. "And you with nothing to say. How 'bout that. Should have had a camera ready."

K.O. just clung to him. Her relief weakened her, and she couldn't wait to call Richard and Abby with the good news. She hadn't realized how much this had weighed on her conscience, and how helpless she had felt to correct the situation until it was suddenly and magically removed. No wonder she hadn't wanted to call them.

"George. You are the best and most perfect person on the face of this earth and I love you dearly."

"I know. You just can't help yourself." He pushed her away and smiled fondly.

"I should get going. I want to call Richard and Abby right away."

"You can call from here."

"I know, but I want to be home. You've helped me once again, and all I've done is drink your booze and publicly malign you."

"At least you're consistent."

K.O. hugged him good-bye, promised to call, and bolted for her car. She had so much to do.

Life was looking up. A little.

The End

ABOUT THE AUTHOR

Victoria Heckman is the award-winning author of the *K.O.'d in Hawai'i Mystery Series*. The second book in this series, *K.O.'d in the Volcano,* is available from Pemberley Press. Her short fiction has appeared in *FUTURES, Short Story, Kid's Highway, Mysterical-e, The Smog, Without a Clue, LoveWords, TRUE SOUL MATES, MORE SLOW DEATH,* and *AND SOME OF THEM ARE DEAD,* and she has published numerous articles and newsletters. She has edited two anthologies, co-edited a third, and is a free-lance editor. She is past president of Sisters in Crime-Central Coast Chapter and is a member of Sisters in Crime National's E Publishing Committee, Mystery Writers of America and the Police Writers Association.

Ms. Heckman divides her time between California and Hawai'i.